G000061412

Donuts and Murder Mystery Collection - Books 1-4

Darlin Donuts Cozy Mini Mystery, Volume 5

J. Somers

Published by J. Somers, 2022.

Donuts and Murder Mini Mystery Collection: Books 1-4

(Darlin Donuts Cozy Mini Mystery)

By J. Somers

Copyright 2020 J. Somers SR

All rights reserved; no part of this publication may be reproduced or transmitted by any means, electronic, mechanical, photocopying or otherwise, without the prior permission of the publisher.

This book is a work of fiction. The names, characters, places, and incidents are products of the writer's imagination or have been used fictitiously. Any resemblance to persons, living or dead is entirely coincidental.

This is a work of fiction. Similarities to real people, places, or events are entirely coincidental.

DONUTS AND MURDER MYSTERY COLLECTION - BOOKS 1-4

First edition. January 19, 2022.

Copyright © 2022 J. Somers.

ISBN: 979-8201677961

Written by J. Somers.

Darlin Donuts Cozy Mini Mystery Collection

Donuts and Murder: The Gossip Columnist

Donuts and Murder: The Mourner

Donuts and Murder: The Rich Housewife

Donuts and Murder: Death by Obituary

Donuts and Murder Short Story: The Gossip Columnist

When a gossip columnist is murdered, Annabelle finds herself caught in the web of suspects.

"Keep calm and eat more donuts."
- Author Unknown

The delicious scent of vanilla and freshly baked donuts wafted to Annabelle Darlin's nose as she pulled the tray of baked vanilla cream donuts out of the oven at her café, Darlin Donuts. Her mouth watered as she inhaled the scrumptious aroma. She couldn't wait to get these items to her loyal customers.

Annabelle loved her new line of work and she loved pleasing her customers who came from all walks of life. Everyone came to the Darlin Donuts Café to hang out and mingle and enjoy delectable treats from the menu.

It wasn't too long ago that Annabelle was in between jobs wondering how on earth she would make ends meet. And when you get to your mid or late thirties, let's face it, you're practically unemployable, competing for jobs with younger people. It was a good thing she had a bit of entrepreneurial savvy in her blood.

It turned out to be a blessing in disguise when Annabelle was suddenly laid off from her job and moved back to the small town of Apple Cove, a town of rolling green hills, apple orchards and the freshest country air you'd ever breathe in, just outside the city of Toronto. Not only did her now ex-boyfriend leave her for their boss—talk about tension mixed with heartbreak, but she escaped the hamster-wheel rat race and used some of the severance pay to open up her own small business, Darlin Donuts café. She had the pleasure of serving the finest customers and being a part of the lives of many wonderful people. Sadly, it wasn't all fun and food when bad things happened—like murder.

Annabelle finished boxing up the treats for Lacie Jones, a columnist with the *Apple Cove Online News*.

When she walked into the dining area to pick up a few napkins, she noticed a man in the corner of the café. He'd been sitting there for a while sipping coffee. There was something off about him.

"Can't believe you're catering to that woman," Aunt Edna said, crocheting, as always. She sat on a chair in the dining area. Earlier she'd been helping Annabelle out but was now taking a well-deserved break. Her fingers seemed to move the speed of light. How did she do it?

"She's a paying customer, Auntie," Annabelle said with a yawn.

"But that woman's mouth runs a mile a minute. Can't say or write anything nice about anyone." Her aunt also yawned. "Darn contagious yawning."

Annabelle grinned. "It's one of life's unexplained mysteries though some scientist think it's something to do with our empathetic response to others."

"Ha. See, I'm empathetic to your feelings."

"Gee, thanks, Aunt Edna."

"Speaking of which, you really need to get more sleep, dear."

"I know. It's just not that easy when you run a business."

"But you have the staff to do everything."

"Still, I have to make sure things run smoothly. Lots of billing and financing behind the scenes, balancing books. You know the fun stuff. I have to be careful when it comes to the money."

"I hear you."

"Speaking of which that gossip woman cost a lot of people money by slandering their business. Make sure you don't disappoint her on her order or she'll do the same to you—even if you don't deserve it."

The man in the corner glanced up for a moment as if interested in their conversation. He then looked back down. He'd been sipping that same cup of coffee for the last hour.

There wasn't many customers in the café that morning since it was a holiday.

"Oh, Auntie. I know she's been quite a character, but let's not be too judgemental. We're running a business here. I'm sure she has a nice side."

"She hides it *very* well."

Of course, Aunt Edna had a good reason for not liking Lacie Jones. Lacie had criticized her boutique once—when Aunt Edna had one. Aunt Edna had owned it with her now ex-husband. It has since closed down. She'd found out that her husband had been a little too friendly with the sales girl—not to mention all the female customers that frequented there.

"I won't be long, Auntie." Annabelle heard the door chime sound and another customer walked into the Darlin Donuts Café.

It was Frank, the sales guy from the Sleep Shop. Speak of the angel.

"Hey there, Annabelle," he said, cheerfully.

"Hey there, yourself, Frank. What's that you've got there?"

"A brochure."

"Cool. Leave it on the counter," she said, yawning. If only she could control her yawning. "I'll get to it later."

"Seems like you can get to it now."

"Why do you say that?"

"You realize that sleep is so important, right?"

"I know, it's how our bodies regenerate and heal through the night. I know."

"Yet, I bet your bed is just ordinary."

"Are we really going to talk about this now?"

"You need to get the latest smart bed."

"Smart bed?"

"My goodness, smart phones, smart TVs, now smart *beds*. Now I know I've heard it all," Aunt Edna said, crocheting and rolling her eyes with the next yarn over.

"Yes, just check it out and let me know. It tracks your sleep, adjusts for comfort, controls the temperature of the bed, plays your favorite songs while you drift off, adjusts the firmness of the mattress, connects to your phone, sets timers, enhances the memory foam and so much more. *This* bed lets you get a good night sleep."

"It had better when you have to figure out how to finance that thing," Aunt Edna said, still crocheting.

Annabelle wondered what her aunt was crocheting this time? She could open up a department store with all the knitted or crochet garments she made.

"Hmm." Annabelle was at a loss for words. "I'll think about that when I get back."

"Okay, let me know."

"Will do, Frank."

She knew what it was like hustling before she opened up her store. Right after she lost her job. Everyone had to survive these days. But did she really need a smart bed? That bed wasn't exactly cheap.

But then neither was she.

She would figure that out later.

Just then, the man in the corner of the café got up and left. There was something odd about him.

Aunt Gabby, Aunt Edna's fraternal twin who also helped out at the café, walked into the dining room from the kitchen wiping her hand on her apron.

"I know who that is," Aunt Gabby said, gesturing to the stranger who just walked out of the café.

"Who?"

"He's the ex-husband of that gossip columnist, Lacie. Some investor."

"Really?"

"Yep! Heard she took him to the cleaners in the divorce. What is he doing in town now?"

"Who knows."

Annabelle thought it was a strange coincidence. She then grabbed the rest of her order and went to her car to deliver her donuts to Lacie.

***

Later, when Annabelle arrived at Lacie's residence, she noticed the front door was slightly ajar.

She jolted when a man stepped out from the side door.

"Oh, you frightened me," Annabelle said, clutching her chest with one hand as she stood holding the box of donuts with her other hand.

"Sorry, I didn't mean to. You're here to see Lacie, right?" he asked, holding the garden hose in his hand. She noticed a scratch, a fresh red mark on his hand.

"Yes, I have her order. I'm from Darlin Donuts."

"Great. She's inside."

"Thank you."

When Annabelle made her way inside, she called out to her client. "Hello. Lacie?"

There was nothing.

She went into what she thought was the living room, but it was a ground-floor bedroom.

"Lacie?"

She glanced over at the massive bed with the glowing lights. The TV was on. Lacie did not look as if she were asleep. The hairs on Annabelle's neck stood to attention.

Lacie looked...dead!

**

After checking Lacie's pulse, Annabelle called 9-1-1. She then tried to do chest compressions, but it was fruitless.

Later, the police arrived on the scene. It didn't take them long to get there.

Lacie's body felt warm, Annabelle noticed. So she must have just died.

Poor thing.

It was good thing they were in a small town and the local ambulance station and hospital were nearby.

Annabelle couldn't help but notice an open laptop on the bed. She quickly took a peek to see if there was anything suspicious there.

Her head started to pound.

Something was wrong.

Something told her that it wasn't a natural death.

There was a cup of coffee on the side table. She glanced at the remaining amount of coffee in it. It seemed as if Lacie didn't have time to finish her morning coffee.

She glanced again at the cup of coffee. A slight headache surfaced at the side of her head. She shook her head and leaned over to the laptop on the bed.

Her eyes then darted to the bed. She found it interesting that Lacie had been working on the bed, yet she had a desk in the corner of her bedroom office.

The chair was an ergonomic office chair. She remembered Lacie always complained about her back. Hence, the ergonomic office chair.

So if the office chair was close to the bed then why work on the bed when her special chair was nearby? Working on the bed would only aggravate her back, wouldn't it?

Something just didn't add up here.

This really bothered Annabelle.

It was as if...

No, she had to stop this. She couldn't suspect any foul play when she had no proof. She really had to stop assuming the worst.

She walked over to the table and felt the cup of coffee. The cup was cold.

She then looked around the room for any signs of suspicious activity.

Well, one thing was for sure, Lacie wasn't hurting for cash. Her room was luxurious. She had upscale furniture and an expensive-looking painting on the wall. The marble floor in her room shined, except for the entrance where people came in and out. But she had a mat there.

She heard a ding and noticed that Lacie had an incoming message on her computer. Annabelle leaned closer then she glanced at the screen of the laptop.

A scandal to end all scandals.

The shocking details of...

Wow, it looked as if Lacie was in the middle of yet another one of her juicy columns. There was a distinctive scent in the room. Perfume? She certainly had expensive taste. Was she expecting a visitor besides Annabelle? Or visitors?

Later, Detective Chad McGuire walked in looking around the room at first. A concerned expression slid across his handsome face. He then rubbed his stubble. It looked as if he'd pulled another all-nighter. Maybe he was just finishing up his night shift and this call came in. He held a coffee in his hand then placed it down on the table.

"Ms. Darlin. Now, why am I not surprised to see you here?" He arched a brow.

"We mustn't keep meeting like this, Cha—I mean Detective McGuire." She'd almost forgotten they weren't alone. The rest of the team were there. She had to remember, even though they'd been a bit chummy lately, especially she helped him to solve a few puzzling murders, they had to keep it professional.

"Can you tell me what happened here?" He walked over to the body and examined it after the forensic team had finished, pulling the white sheet from Lacie's face then covering her again.

"Well, she called to order a dozen donuts for her meeting this morning and..." Annabelle's voice choked.

"I'm sorry," Detective Chad's voice was soft.

He knew how hard it was for her seeing her customer like that. Especially given it was not the first time a customer of hers had been found dead—and she'd been the one to stumble on the body.

"Did you see anything suspicious?" he continued, as he pulled out his pen and notepad.

"Well, the door was open for one thing. The gardener told me to go right in."

"We already spoke to the gardener."

"Okay."

Annabelle thought for a moment. She was about to say something else then changed her mind.

"Annabelle, is something wrong?" Detective Chad asked, a curious expression on his face.

"Well," she said, walking around. "Don't you find it odd that she was sitting up on the bed typing?"

"Not really. Lots of people do that, Annabelle. It looks as if she could have had a heart attack, but the coroners will verify the cause of death. Are you telling me you suspect foul play?" He arched a brow.

"Well, something just seems a bit off. She always complained about a bad back. Why sit up in the bed and type?"

"Annabelle."

Just then Annabelle noticed something on the laptop. She glanced at the screen. The article she was working on had today's date. And it was time stamped.

"See here?" Detective Chad said, looking at the screen of the laptop. "Seems like she was working on an article for her blog and she even dated and put the time on it."

"Detective, could you do me a favor and look at the time the article was originally written. I don't want to touch the laptop for obvious reasons."

"Of course, we'll look into that too, Annabelle. But trust me, I don't think this is what you think it is. Besides, even if the document was created on a different day, as I suspect that's what you're thinking, she could have easily started a new post in an old template."

"True, but..."

"No evidence of forced entry, sir," another officer said to Detective Chad.

"Thanks, Pete," Chad said, before turning back to Annabelle.

Before she could say anything else, more members of the forensic team came in once again and the coroners came for the body. That was Annabelle's cue to leave.

**

As Annabelle walked out of the house, she turned around and took a quick observation of the window and the door and stood back examining the front porch.

No sign of forced entry, eh?

You mean no obvious *sign of forced entry.*

Something did not sit too well with her.

"Unbelievable," an older woman startled Annabelle and she spun around.

The woman had curlers in her hair, as she stood outside her home, next door to Lacie's. The woman had a coffee in her hand.

"Excuse me?" Annabelle said. There were police vehicles everywhere and neighbors were out on the street gawking and chatting amongst each other over their picket fences.

"I'm Mavis, her neighbor."

"I'm Annabelle."

"Oh, right. You're the donut lady. I love Darlin Donuts."

"Thank you. Um, you were saying?"

"Can't believe her past caught up with her," the woman said, sipping her coffee as if nothing out of the ordinary happened.

"Are you talking about Lacie?"

"Oh, yes. We all know her around here. I mean we all *knew* her. She was a busy body, she was. Rest her soul. She would always be chatting with everyone and sharing a bit of juicy news. But she was a talker. Talking everybody's business like it was *her* business."

"I take it you were not a close friend."

"Oh, no. I had nothing against her. But..." The woman looked around to see if anyone else was listening. "Well, let's just say, she was gentleman's lady. I had nothing to worry about, of course. I didn't have a husband for her to take." The woman chuckled and sipped her coffee again.

Okay. This was awkward.

Annabelle didn't want to engage in any gossip. But she wanted to get to the bottom of what really happened to her customer, Lacie.

"Are you saying you suspect one of her...dates..."

"Oh no. Nothing like that."

"Did you see anything suspicious this morning?" Annabelle jumped to ask. She figured this had to be the ultimate neighborhood watch community. Since everybody was watching each other—in more ways than one.

If Annabelle didn't know any better, she'd swear she was on Gossip Boulevard, the street of talkers. In fact, wasn't that the nickname of the street? There was another gossip columnist on the street if Annabelle remembered correctly, wasn't there?

The woman sipped her coffee again, pondering.

"Well, you know she had a reputation as a widow spider as they call 'em. You know. Marry and then her husbands end up dead before the first anniversary. She's been married like..." Mavis looked up as if counting sheep in the sky. "Oh, I don't know, I think she might have been on marriage number seven."

"Seven?"

"Oh, yes. And they each left her a nice life insurance policy. This isn't even her only home."

"It isn't?" Annabelle took mental note. She would have to share this information with Detective Chad soon.

"Oh, no. She has a villa in Spain, a lovely piece of beachfront property in Florida. Oh, this woman takes the most expensive trips several times a year. And you should see her Louis Vuitton luggage. Amazing."

"I can imagine. Listen, have you spoken to the police as yet?"

"Oh, yes, an officer spoke to me earlier."

"I see. Well, I'll be seeing you around," Annabelle said, as a thought struck her. She had to get back to the café now and when she got a moment, she was going to do a little sleuthing online. Something just did not add up.

**

"Oh dear, please tell me she wasn't poisoned by one of our donuts," Aunt Gabby said, as she helped Annabelle in the kitchen an hour later.

"No, Aunt Gabby. Nothing like that. I hadn't even delivered the donuts to her when I found her. And she had no food around. Just a cup of..." Annabelle paused for a moment."

"What is it dear?"

"Oh, nothing. I don't know what happened to her. They said it looks like she had a heart attack. Her body was still warm and no one saw anyone leave or enter this morning. She was all alone."

"But?" Aunt Edna said, crocheting a new cardigan, as always, as she seated herself in the corner of the office at the back of the Darlin Donuts Café.

"But what?"

"Oh, please, darling niece, I know you suspect something."

"Well, it does seem a bit off."

Annabelle searched online for Lacie's social media profile to see her last posts. Luckily, Jack was in the kitchen taking care of everything. She had a competent and professional team working for Darlin Donuts. This freed up a bit of her time, though she loved to go out and meet customers by delivering their special orders.

"Find anything?" Aunt Gabby asked.

"Nope. Not yet."

Annabelle then landed on Lacie's social media page.

She immediately peeked at her friends list. For some reason her eyes were drawn to it. She had five thousand friends. Luckily, her profile was set to public. Or maybe that had been *unlucky* for Lacie.

"Look here," Annabelle said.

"What is it, dear?"

"Looks as if Lacie made the news herself. Here's an article about marriage number seven. That was last year."

Annabelle looked carefully, the author of the article showed a snapshot of Lacie's marriages or her destination weddings.

"So she would go off to the Caribbean and marry these poor unsuspecting fellows. Then dump 'em when the honeymoon was over and move on to the next. I heard about people like that. They just love the celebration of the day, not the actual marriage. It's like she's addicted to weddings!" Aunt Edna commented.

"No, no. I don't think it's quite like that. I mean, they all died," Annabelle said.

"Yes, mysteriously, too."

She looked at each of the men in the pictures. They were all tall, middle aged, handsome men, greying at the sides. They all looked similar in their traits. Annabelle guessed she went for the tall, dark and handsome types. With money.

And to think, they were each married and left their wives for her. Except one, she noted from the article. One of them was widowed.

**

The following day, the Darlin Donuts café was filled with chatter about the latest death in the community.

"Well, that's one less busy body with a big mouth," one patron commented.

"Sad to hear she's gone, but that woman could gossip. Oh, well. I guess her number was up."

Only, Annabelle thought it was more than simply a death.

But what if she was wrong this time?

Was she thinking into this too much? Then why was she getting a headache? She always had headaches when something was off.

Her auntie was right. Maybe she should have that checked out.

Just then Detective Chad came in through the front door, sounding the door chime, and her heart galloped in her chest.

Okay, why did that always happen whenever she saw Chad?

She had to remind herself that nothing could come of anything with Chad. Besides, she was still on a break from dating right now. She had to keep reminding herself. But, oh, he was eye candy, with that sexy stubble and run-your-fingers-through dark mousy hair.

"Hey stranger," she said to him as he neared the counter.

"Hey yourself, Ms. Darlin."

"Any more news?"

"Well, nothing I can talk about right now."

"Can I get you anything?"

"Sure, how about five minutes."

"Five minutes? What kind of donut is that? We don't have that on the menu."

He grinned. "Seriously, do you have a minute? Can we talk privately?"

"Sure. I'll have one of the cashiers take over."

Moments later, they were in her back office.

"Spoke to my boss at the department. He knows how much you've helped on the other cases, so I'm just asking you again, did you see anything suspicious?"

"Why?"

"Asked you first."

"Asked you second."

He gave her a raised brow and a sweet grin on his lips.

"Fine. There is something that's off and I can't quite pin my finger on it. I wish I could."

"Okay, you said she called in and asked for a dozen donuts for her meeting this morning?"

"That's right."

"How did she sound to you?"

"Well, that's just it. I didn't actually take the call. She texted it."

"She did?"

"Yes."

"I see."

"What is it?"

"Well, she did have a heart attack."

"Oh. When did she die?"

"The body was still warm when we got there, so we're just waiting to hear back from the coroner."

"I see."

"I can see the wheels turning in that amazing brain of yours, Ms. Darlin."

"She must have had surveillance cameras. A woman like that would want to secure her property. She had so much money in the bank." Annabelle didn't want to spread gossip but wondered if she should just tell Chad what she'd heard from Mavis, the neighbor. She decided it could help to find out what really happened to Lacie, since she truly felt foul play was at hand.

A woman like that with so many enemies? Having seven husbands whom she'd taken from wives, didn't make her popular with at least seven women. Not to mention, her gossip site which drew much criticism.

"Can I have a look at the footage. I might be able to help you out there."

"Okay, I'll check with the boss. I don't see that being a problem though since you have a lot of customers in the community and might recognize something strange."

That's what she was afraid of. But she had to find out what really happened to Lacie and she didn't think it was just a heart attack.

**

Annabelle scrolled through the security footage. A cup of hot steaming coffee in her hand. Something she really needed right now.

Then it dawned on her again. That cup of coffee. Something was odd about the one in Lacie's room.

"See anyone odd?" Chad asked.

"Well," she said, glancing at footage of people on the video. "There's the delivery guy this morning. Then he was there last night too. Why was the delivery guy there again? I guess she had a lot of packages delivered to her. And of course, Frank was peddling some sales pamphlets to her. So were a few others, including her neighbor, Mavis!"

What had Mavis been doing there last night?

"Yes, but we're not concerned with anyone who went to her house last night since she died this morning."

"Hmm."

"So, we have over a dozen people who were around her in the last twenty-four hours. If you want to count this morning, at least three, including the delivery person."

Annabelle thought for a moment.

There went her head again.

Something was off and she just couldn't pin point it.

Just then the sergeant came into Chad's office. He went over to the window and pulled the blinds open. The glare of the sun shone in and the screen of the TV monitor glared.

"Boss, you mind closing the blinds again."

"That's it!" Lacie said.

"Excuse me?"

"The blinds."

The sergeant and Detective Chad gave Annabelle a puzzling look.

"I know what happened to Lacie. She was murdered!"

**

"You wanted to meet me *here*?" the man said, looking around as if he were creeped out to be back in Lacie's room at her house.

"Yes, I just wanted to ask you a few questions."

"Shoot. Go ahead."

"Why did you see Lacie last night?"

"Excuse me?" he said, his expression numb with shock.

"You were the last one to see her last night, according to surveillance cameras."

"Oh, no. You're not pinning this on me. I didn't murder her."

"Who said anything about murder? I didn't mention any such thing."

He narrowed his eyes. Sweat beaded his forehead.

"Annabelle. Come on. It's me."

"Yes, I know it's you. That's what gave me a heartache about the whole thing. You were always the sweet salesman or the delivery guy or any other gig you could get your hands on. I noticed the resemblance to your father. One of Lacie's ex, now late husband. She inherited his fortune. I checked it out. And well, the fact that you're struggling doing any little gig you could get, meant that she probably didn't share anything with you. When a widower marries, if he dies, it all goes to his new bride automatically, not to his children with the caveat that the surviving new spouse would do the right thing and share with his children. Or child in this case. Only Lacie didn't, did she Frank."

He swallowed hard. He was about to break.

"I didn't mean to...it..."

"But you used to work at the lab part time, cleaning up. You had access to potassium chloride which could mimic a heart attack."

"How did you guess?" He looked amazed at Annabelle.

"A few things. The coffee was cold. It should have been steaming hot or even warm when I came in. Then she was on the bed, seemingly working on an article. But when I checked her previous salacious articles, I realized she'd already published that one. You just set it up to look as if she were working on it. And Lacie never worked on the bed. She had a bad back. That's why she set up that ergonomic chair in the corner of her room."

"That's how you knew?"

"No. I thought it was strange that you were here last night, unless you were checking up on a customer. Lacie has the new smart bed. You could easily set the timer on the bed to keep warm, Frank."

He slapped his palm to his forehead.

"You set the bed to warm to heat it up so it would throw off the time of death," Annabelle said. "I couldn't understand why the body was warm and the coffee was cold. It was because the coffee was from *last night*. Not this morning. And...the blinds."

"The what?"

"The blinds. It was a sunny morning. And Lacie always drew open the blinds. Yet, it was closed. Why? Because she died last night. She would have opened it in the morning. But she didn't live to see the morning. Everyone who was interviewed by police said the blinds were closed this morning, just as I had seen."

"I hated her. She married my father. It's as if she researched all the new rich men in the area. My father never gave me much. But I knew that I would inherit the house I grew up in when he kicked the bucket. Only he married that...that woman. I knew she'd get everything. But I thought she'd give me the house. Instead she put it up for sale. Why did she do that? What did it matter to her. She had so many homes she's collected through her marriages and investments. I just wanted the home I grew up in with the memories of my family. But that witch took it all away from me. I hated her."

"So her smart bed ended up being her *death* bed. You didn't have to kill her, Frank." Annabelle's voice was soft. "You sent me the text from her phone, didn't you?"

"Yeah, I did."

"Oh, Frank," she shook her head, in disappointment.

"I'm not sorry I got rid of her." He squared his shoulders. "I'm glad I got that off my chest."

"Yes, murder is a burden to carry on the conscience."

"So what now?"

"A confession—which I have recorded."

He looked defeated.

Annabelle felt sorry for him. But he murdered a woman in cold blood. His step-mother. He had to serve his time.

Not soon after, Detective Chad came in, amazement on his face as the other members of his team read Frank his rights and arrested him for the murder of Lacie, his stepmother.

**

"I can't believe I let you talk me into that, Annabelle," Detective Chad said later.

"But it worked, didn't it. I knew Frank. He's..."

"Please don't say harmless, Annabelle, he just murdered a woman in cold blood."

"No, I wasn't going to say that. But you're right."

"We were ready and waiting to storm right in."

"I know. And thank you, Detective. But I needed to get that confession out of him."

"What is it with you?" He grinned. "You have some serious thrill issues. But it's dangerous, Annabelle. Even if you think you know someone, people can change in a heartbeat and never mind that survival mechanism. People would resort to anything to protect themselves. Remember that?"

"Oh, I will, Detective. I will."

"And, uh..." He hesitated for a moment. "You want to grab a bite to eat."

"Detective, are you asking me out on a date?"

"Well..."

"I would love to."

***

Donuts and Murder Short Story: The Mourner

When her oldest and wealthiest customer dies, Annabelle finds herself caught in the middle of an inheritance feud which leads to murder.

"For an eighty-five-year-old, he sure has a lot of guests," Aunt Edna said to Annabelle Darlin as she looked around the lavishly decorated memorial room.

They had just finished setting up the refreshments for the memorial of one of Darlin Donuts' oldest and dearest customers, Mr. Lion.

"Why does that surprise you, Auntie?"

"Well, for starters, I had no idea he had so many friends and family. He always complained no one came to visit him. Didn't he refer to himself as a *loner*? He was pretty much a recluse."

"Yes, you're right about that."

Annabelle thought carefully for a moment. She turned around and observed all the faces of those in attendance. Many of them were younger. There were a few elders there but then she supposed many of his closer friends would have died from old age. That happened when you got to a certain age.

But she couldn't help but have a sinking feeling in the pit of her stomach. She truly hoped they were not all there for his money.

Why was the room filled with young people and Mr. Lion had no children or grandchildren?

He was rumored to be the richest resident in the town when he was alive, and probably the richest man in the country. The man was not a big spender, but he was a generous tipper to all who encountered him professionally.

And he would often talk about his stocks whenever he had the chance. He also took to social media, strangely enough. He opened a social media account for his collectible items. Especially his lucrative coin collection and rare art originals that could easily fetch in the millions or even billions. Luckily, he never mentioned where he lived on social media or else he could have been a target for thieves, but still it was risky.

When he was alive, he always complained about being alone. The only time he was ever surrounded by people was at the Darlin Donuts Caféé. He once told her how much he enjoyed the family-like atmosphere of her donut shop.

It turned out to be a blessing in disguise when Annabelle was suddenly laid off from her job and moved back to the small town of Apple Cove, a town of rolling green hills, apple orchards and the freshest country air you'd ever breathe in, just outside the city of Toronto. Not only did her now ex-boyfriend leave her for their boss—talk about tension mixed with heartbreak, but she escaped the hamster-wheel rat race and used some of the severance pay to open up her own small business, Darlin Donuts café. She had the pleasure of serving the finest customers and being a part of the lives of many wonderful people. Sadly, it wasn't all fun and food when bad things happened—like murder.

Annabelle noticed the deceased elder had the most expensive-looking watch on his wrist. A gold watch that sparkled. He was dressed in a pristine expensive-looking suit in the coffin.

Oh, well, might as well dress his best for his final appearance. He looked so peaceful and asleep.

In fact, there was a smug grin on his lips, if she was not mistaken. The casket was open as per his request. He probably wanted to show off all his bling.

She supposed he had requested from the mortician to have it that way as he'd planned everything down to the last detail.

His former part-time housekeeper, who came in on weekends, told Annabelle earlier that he had a lot of strange requests, including the catering to be done by Darlin Donuts, his favorite place to eat and that all the guests should be given donuts and coffee.

"Thank you for catering our grandfather's service," a young man with dark brown hair in a black suit said as he walked over to Annabelle. He was roguishly handsome and looked as if he hadn't slept in days. Beside him was another man with blond hair and green eyes. He also looked sorrowful, but said nothing.

"Oh, no problem," Annabelle said.

"I'm Pete, his grandson." He extended his hand. "And this is my brother, Liam."

"Nice to meet you two. My deepest condolence," she added.

She didn't want to say anything but she was stunned to learn that Mr. Lion even had grandsons. She thought he never had any kids of his own.

He certainly never mentioned any family to Annabelle. And oftentimes Mr. Lion would be at the caféé talking a lot about his life. As if he wanted others to know him in some way. Why on earth didn't Pete or Liam visit him before?

Mr. Lion mentioned he never even had visitors to his home.

He was an eccentric man who did things differently. He dressed rather unique for an older gentleman. And he had his pride. He would tell stories about his travels all over the world and how popular he was on social media. Though he would spend his evenings alone, save for the Internet being his friend.

But as Aunt Edna would say, it's nice to have friends online on the internet, but it's more important to have friends in *real life* too.

Annabelle glanced around again after Pete and Liam went to take a seat in the front pew in front of the coffin.

She wondered how many of the guests were online friends and how many were his friends offline, if any.

She noticed Pete and Liam didn't really talk to anyone else there. No one came up to them to offer their condolence.

How strange?

The world was a strangely different place these days. No one knew each other. Even if they had their contacts in their phones, who would have the password to reach those contacts at a time like this? Most people had friends in cyberspace but not in real life which was not necessarily a good thing.

Just then a shapely young woman walked into the memorial room with a black tight-fitting dress and she wore a veil over her face. Who was she?

Annabelle smelled her strong designer perfume before she even entered the room. Her blond hair was tied up into a bun and she wore a large rimmed black hat with a black rose on it.

"Oh, my Al. Al," she wailed, as she walked close to the coffin. She then hugged the coffin.

"Oh, no. No. No. Why? Why?" she wailed out.

"He was eighty-five," Aunt Edna whispered to Annabelle. "I mean, that's not the worst age in the world to go, is it?"

"Aunt Edna, please," Annabelle whispered back.

"Sorry, niece. I was just saying. She's behaving as if it's the funeral of a five year old not an eighty-five year old. A bit over the top, isn't she?"

Annabelle quickly took a peek of the guest book nearby in which the woman signed the most recent entry.

She noticed the mourner's name was Lucy.

The other guests didn't seem too bothered by all the wailing. In fact, they didn't show much emotion at all.

Just then the head usher, whom they'd met earlier when they needed directions to the chapel, went over to Lucy and politely asked her to be seated.

It was an upscale lovely memorial home that was known for performing elite services, especially for those who did not belong to a church. The fresh scent of cut flowers and pine was evident in the air.

Annabelle also noticed the expensive-looking oak and velvet seats and plush carpet. It was a serene environment.

"Do you notice something, Auntie?" Annabelle spoke softly as they sat near the back where the refreshments were.

"That Ms. Crying's dress is too tight and she's having problems sitting?"

"No, no. Not that. Auntie, please be nice. You promised."

"Fine. Fine."

"Don't you see that most of the guests are, well, young."

"So? Most of his friends probably died of old age. And it looks like he must have had a child who gave him the grandsons. Apparently, they weren't that close."

"I didn't know he *had* any children. He never mentioned them. And he had many followers on his social media page. But..." Something was bothering Annabelle, but after one of the guests turned around, she stilled her tongue.

After the lovely service, in which the crying-in-the-tight-dress lady turned out to be the deceased's girlfriend to the chagrin and surprise of his grandsons, the guests gathered to have their refreshments.

Mr. Lion had asked to be buried in Texas beside his first wife, so his body would be flown down south of the border.

Annabelle walked to the front of the room to pick up one of the serving trays which was now empty. She wasn't sure how it got there, but it was a Darlin Donuts tray and she didn't want to leave a mess there.

When she moved closer to the casket, her jaw fell open.

She couldn't help but notice that the sparkling gold watch was missing from Mr. Lion's wrist. Her heart jolted.

Who could have taken it?

What happened to it?

"Mmm, these donuts are delicious," a guest said, interrupting her thoughts.

For a moment, Annabelle beamed with pride. Well, at least she did her part to provide comforting treats for the mourners.

"I cannot believe he was dating that young drama queen," another guest said. "Can you believe they were dating?"

Annabelle recognized the woman as Mr. Lion's neighbor. She was talking to someone else in what was an attempt at a quiet voice, only Annabelle could hear every word. It wasn't appropriate to be having such discussions, Annabelle thought to herself as she stood behind the serving table while everyone helped themselves to their treats.

"It was good that he had everything paid for in advance," Aunt Edna said. "He couldn't rely on anyone else making sure he had a good turnout and a decent place for a memorial."

"Yes, especially when you get to a certain age, it gives you peace of mind knowing that your loved ones don't have to worry about these things..." Annabelle paused for a moment and saw that over by the far corner, Mr. Lion's grandson and Mr. Lion's girlfriend were having a heated argument.

What on earth were they arguing about? Especially at a time like this?

"You're a gold digger! And you're not getting a penny of my grandfather's money!" he charged.

The guests spun around shocked with whispers and mumblings. "What a disgrace," another guest said.

"Now you see here. This is why I don't like going to funerals. So much drama," Aunt Edna said. "If it were up to me I wouldn't even attend my own."

"Auntie! Shh!" Annabelle whispered, flushed.

Heat climbed to Annabelle's cheeks. She felt sorry for Mr. Lion, even though he was dead. But this was supposed to be his memorial, not some family feud session.

"No wonder he hardly spoke about you," Lucy, Mr. Lion's girlfriend, said to his grandson. "You're just after his money. You never cared about him."

Lucy huffed, glanced around realizing that they were being overheard and she finally said, "I'm leaving."

She turned on her high heels almost stumbling at first. Another gentleman caught her fall. She then spun around on her heels and stormed out.

Well, so much for a peaceful gathering. Annabelle had a sinking feeling that something awful was about to happen.

**

"Excuse me?" Annabelle said over the phone to the lawyer on Monday morning. She sat in her office at the Darlin Donuts Cáféé. "You need me to be at your office for the reading of Mr. Lion's will?"

"Yes, Ma'am. Your presence is requested."

The lawyer then gave Annabelle the address to which she wrote down the information.

When she got off the phone, her aunt, who just walked into her office, couldn't help but notice Annabelle's stunned expression.

"Everything all right, dear?" Aunt Edna asked.

"I don't know," Annabelle said, dazed. "Mr. Lion's lawyer just called and asked if I could come in to see him this morning regarding the reading of his will."

"What? Mr. Lion left you something in his will?"

"I have no idea, Auntie. I guess we'll have to see. He was a lovely customer and we always got along, but I'm surprised as much as you are that he mentioned me. I feel honored..." *And a little shocked.*

Annabelle was certainly not looking forward to seeing Mr. Lion's extravagant younger girlfriend, nor his estranged grandsons.

She could just imagine how this was going to turn out.

Later that morning, Annabelle showed up at the law office.

"Nice to see you again," Pete said to Annabelle.

Was he being sarcastic? If he was, he certainly hid it well in his charming voice. What must he think of her? The caterer, owner of a donut shop, was listed in his wealthy grandfather's will.

"I'm surprised your grandfather mentioned my name in his will," Annabelle told him. "Where's your brother?"

"Oh, Lance. He couldn't make it."

Lance?

"He couldn't *make* it?" Annabelle was stunned.

And wait a minute? Wasn't his brother's name *Liam*? Why did Pete refer to him as Lance? Or perhaps Lance was his brother's real name.

"Okay, everyone take a seat," the lawyer said as he entered the room.

It was a large office with a library of hundreds of law books in leather bound covers and a beautiful view of the lake.

Annabelle glanced out the window and saw the breathtaking lake. She could see a few cars parked below, a woman walking her dog, and a hot dog stand. It was a picturesque view on a sunny Monday morning. It was a nice law office in a quiet area of town filled with parks.

Annabelle noticed that Mr. Lion's neighbors were there too. So was his part-time weekend housekeeper, Mrs. Jones. And of course, Lucy, Mr. Lion's much younger girlfriend. She had a smug grin on her lips for some reason and had her nose held up high and her arms folded defensively across her chest.

"To my dear housekeeper, Mrs. Jones, I leave my artwork above the fireplace, the one you so greatly admire every day," the lawyer read.

The lawyer continued to read on as Mr. Lion requested certain pieces of art to be left to different individuals.

She could see that Pete was getting uncomfortable as he shifted in his seat. He fiddled with his necktie several times and beads of sweat surfaced on his face.

"And last but not least, to my darling fiancée Lucy. I leave everything else."

"What?" Pete stood up. "This is crazy!"

"Ha! He didn't even mention you in his will. See? He cared for you as much as you cared for him. Out of my way," Lucy said getting up.

"You're not getting away with this!" Pete yelled. "I'm going to contest the will."

The lawyer then continued as he wasn't quite finished and seemed unmoved by this display of drama. "And lastly, anyone who contests this will gets nothing," he finished.

Pete's jaw fell wide open and the look of shock spread across his face. He looked as if all the blood had drained from his body.

He stormed out of the office in a rage.

Annabelle wished she wasn't there at the moment. The last thing she needed was to witness all of this.

Annabelle was grateful that Mr. Lion left her a lovely expensive painting to put in the Darlin Donuts' dining room. She would put it up on display as soon as she got hold of it. The customers would love it!

But why did Mr. Lion leave nothing to his grandsons?

About ten minutes later, after the paperwork was sorted out, Annabelle heard two shots fired outside.

Everyone jumped and ran to the window.

"Oh, no! Is that Lucy? She's been shot! Call 9-1-1!" Annabelle looked and saw a blue sedan drive off towards the west.

Lucy was laying there on the pavement beside a car. Was it *Lucy's* car?

They all hurried down and out of the small building towards the parking lot and to where Lucy lay still.

Annabelle thought about the car that sped the scene moments earlier. It was a navy blue sedan, she said to herself committing it to memory. The car also looked familiar. Annabelle thought she saw it at the memorial home parking lot on the day of Mr. Lion's funeral, but she could not be sure. Just then her head ached.

Annabelle wished she'd gotten a view of the license plates, but she was too far away when she first heard the shots and the car sped off.

She looked at the body.

Lucy was dead. There were no two ways about it. She'd been shot in the head. She was gone.

It was almost like a hit.

Annabelle had heard two gun shots fired earlier. She couldn't tell if Lucy had been hit once or twice, but either way, it was horrific.

What an awful way to go.

She couldn't help but notice Lucy's expensive-looking designer bag tossed to the side from the impact of the fall. Annabelle reached down to pick it up.

Annabelle observed that Lucy had a passport in her bag. And some printed out plane tickets. Or was that one ticket?

Lucy also had wads of cash in her designer handbag rolled up. And a business card.

The card read:

In Good Company

The irony of it all. She certainly wasn't in good company a moment ago.

Sirens sounded off in the distance. Thank goodness the cops were on their way. Or was that an ambulance?

**

The police were on the scene in no time. Well, this was not a catering event, but nonetheless, what must Detective Chad think of Annabelle, always there at the scene of a crime? A murder.

Just then Annabelle noticed Liam, Pete's brother there. What was he doing there? Didn't Pete say Liam couldn't make the reading this morning?

She saw a witness point to Liam. And overheard the witness telling an officer that the man with the gun shot the woman because she stole his inheritance or something to that fact.

An officer took the gun from Liam and Liam was read his rights and arrested on the spot after being asked a few questions. Annabelle overhead someone saying that Liam had fake ID on him.

What was going on?

There was more drama and commotion on the street than she'd ever seen before in her life. Forget reality TV or a soap opera. This was absolutely unbelievable!

Crowds soon gathered on the once quiet street to see what was going on. Many onlookers pulled out their cell phones to record. What was this world coming to?

"I didn't do it," Liam was heard yelling.

He really should take the advice of the officer to remain silent since anything he said could be used against him.

But there was something in his tone that made Annabelle believe him. It was just a gut instinct.

"It's not my gun. I just picked it up, I swear," Liam was heard shouting again as another officer guided him into the back of the police cruiser with his hands cuffed behind his back. He'd been read his rights moments earlier after police questioned him and found the gun on him. It was illegal for a casual civilian to own firearm in Ontario in any case. That alone might have gotten him arrested.

"Looks like we meet again, Detective," Annabelle said as the handsome detective Chad MaGuire, with his gorgeous stubble approached her.

"Yes, it looks that way, Ms. Darlin. Annabelle," he corrected himself after seeing her expression. She always told him to call her Annabelle. But she was also aware of how professional he had to be and follow procedures. They'd had lunch once. An experience she'd never forget. He was charming, when he wasn't tired from overwork.

"Can you tell me what happened here?" he asked.

She was still stunned that Liam or Lance or whatever his name was, was arrested for the murder of Lucy, his grandfather's fiancée.

Annabelle told the detective everything that happened. All she knew.

"I see," he said writing down some notes.

She told the detective that she didn't really witness the murder. She only heard two shots fired soon after Lucy left the lawyer's office.

"So she inherited everything in the will?" Detective Chad asked, clarifying. He seemed as if he were in disbelief. "And nothing for his grandsons? Is that correct?"

"Yes," she said, almost regretting it later. But she had to tell the truth. There was nothing she could do about that. However, it just gave Liam a perfect motive.

Money.

Money was among the top motives for murder, wasn't it?

Money.

Revenge.

Greed.

Sex.

Self-Defense.

Secrets.

Power.

She didn't think it had anything to do with self-defense. Or sex, but she could be wrong about that. Secrets? She wasn't so sure. But revenge and money might be the top motivators in this case.

In this case, she believed it could be more than just money. Something just wasn't adding up here. But what was it?

**

"What do you think happened?" Aunt Edna asked the next day at the Darlin Donuts café.

"Well, almost everything was left to Lucy. I'm sure his grandsons didn't like that."

"So you think Liam killed her. But then if you kill someone you can't inherit from them, isn't that right?"

"Yes, but she wasn't the original estate owner. I'm sure it's a bit more complicated than that." Annabelle thought hard for a moment. "I showed the business card to Detective Chad. I wonder if he's going to follow up on it."

"I'm sure he will."

"But what if he doesn't? They think they have their guy."

"Liam already confessed to it."

"He did?" Annabelle was astonished.

"Yes, I heard about it this morning. They're keeping him inside until a bail hearing could be arranged."

"You don't think he'd get bail do you?"

"Apparently, it was her gun. And he said it was self-defense."

Annabelle's head began to pound. Something wasn't right. Why would he confess to the crime? She was so sure he was sincere yesterday when he shouted he didn't do it.

**

Annabelle had a bit of sleuthing to do on her own before bothering the cops with her suspicions—just in case she was on a trail colder than a slice of cucumber. She just didn't want to waste their time. But she also remembered what Chad said about not getting involved for her own safety.

She knew it was dangerous. She should just leave it to the cops. But...

She sat in her office at the back of the kitchen at the donut shop and called *In Good Company* but the line was busy. She decided to hold off for now and would try the number again later.

Annabelle then went online to Lucy's social media page while in the office.

Her aunt came into the back room office. "Don't tell me you're going online to search for information again." Aunt Edna had her hands on her hips. "You're a social media sleuth!"

Social Media Sleuth?

Was she wrong for liking that term?

Truth be told, it looked as if making tasty donuts, mingling with her wonderful customers, and hanging out on social media living vicariously through others seemed to be her thing these days.

"Auntie, you'd be surprised what you can learn about a person on social media. They post everything. Sometimes too much. By the way, prospective employers often search a person's social media page to see what type of person they are before hiring."

"Why surely you're not planning on hiring that Lucy girl. She's dead!"

"No, no. Of course not. I'm just saying that when people post their lives publicly, it can be seen by anyone. The trick is to notice useful information. In this case, useful information that could help track down the killer who took Lucy's life! I'm sure she would want justice to be done."

"Obviously."

"Everyone posts online these days."

"They put their whole life online, don't they?"

"Nothing wrong with sharing with your friends but when your feed is public it can get a bit unsafe. For instance, do you know there are many people who post their date of birth and the names of their pets or mother's maiden name?"

Aunt Edna gasped.

"That's right," Annabelle continued. "Any criminal can guess their passcodes or passwords from that information alone since too many people use it because it's easy to remember."

"Or any amateur sleuth like yourself can pick up on clues that are right in their face."

Annabelle shook her head and playfully rolled her eyes.

"Oh! Look here," Annabelle said, looking at Lucy's social media page.

"What is it?"

"The social media groups she's a member of. She posts about them here."

Her aunt's jaw fell wide open again. "How to find a rich man? Well, you can't get any more direct than that."

"Rich Dates. Wealth Attraction. Sugar Dating."

One of the sites listed mentioned that it was a two-way street. You provide companionship in exchange for being taken care of.

"Well she has a lot on display."

"But it's what she does *not* have on display that concerns me, Auntie," Annabelle said, studying the screen.

"Like what?"

"Being engaged. She mentions a lot about being lonely and single and searching, yet she was engaged to a wealthy man. Yet, no mention of him or being engaged or anything. Yet, he left an entire fortune to her including a massive house.

I just don't get it." Annabelle's pulse pounded and her head throbbed.

"Okay, to be fair, some people feel comfortable posting about some aspects of their lives while keeping other things private," Annabelle continued. "I get that. But it just doesn't seem consistent with her personality online and I'm getting a strong pulsing headache."

"You need a pain killer, honey."

"I need to find the truth. It's killing me."

"The stress will kill you if you don't leave it be. Let the cops handle it."

She then looked at *In Good Company's* profile.

"Look here," Annabelle said.

"What is it?"

"Lucy was an actress."

"I see. Well, she certainly got herself a good part in Mr. Lion's will."

"No, no. Not just that. Look at some of these pictures she posted."

Aunt Edna glanced at the screen. "Yes, she's taken a lot of trips to the beach."

"But look at that person there. Do you recognize him?"

"Not really. He looks like a blur."

Annabelle looked closer. "I think I know who it is. And yet he pretended he didn't know her. And I think I know whose car sped off that day she was shot."

It was all coming together, Annabelle's heart leaped in her chest. But there was one more piece of the puzzle she had to be sure of.

"Thank you for calling In Good Company, how can I help you?" the woman answered the other end of the phone when Annabelle tried the number again.

"Hi, I just found your business card. I hope I've called the right company. What is it that you do?"

There was a pause on the end of the phone.

"Well, Ma'am we provide guests."

"Guests?"

"Yes, Ma'am. Extras for social functions."

**

"How did you guess?" The man standing before Annabelle looked smug.

"Well, I checked with the company and found out they provided actresses and actors to play the part in weddings, memorials, and parties as crowds or guests. It made sense since many of the guests didn't know each other at Mr. Lion's funeral."

"Nothing unusual about that?"

"When I asked the company if Mr. Lion hired them they told me no. It was you, wasn't it?"

"So?"

"Mr. Lion didn't have any children or grandchildren. I thought it was Pete, but he was a detective on your trail. He only assumed the role of the grandson and you tried to frame him not knowing where he was from since you had a guest list already. I saw you scanning it at the memorial which I thought was odd. You had your eyes on Pete and Liam wondering who they were since Mr. Lion confided in you, unfortunately, about the fact that he had no one. Sadly, a big mistake on his part."

"Well, you can't prove any of this had anything to do with Lucy's murder."

"Oh, it has everything to do with it. You see social media reveals a lot about people. Including selfies. Even though she wore a disguise, she had many images of herself on social media including some with you. And I thought, what a coincidence that she knows you. Then there was the car speeding off. It was the first car I saw when I arrived earlier ahead of the guests, which meant it belonged to someone who works at the memorial home. You."

He chuckled humorlessly.

"Then the bit about her passport and ticket for one person. She was going to double cross you and take all the money and leave. You didn't want any of the money to go to you or it would look suspicious, especially with the detectives on your case...so you arranged to have it in your girlfriend's name. Only she was going to double cross you. You were outside waiting for her. I saw your car when I was looking out the window at the lake in the lawyer's office."

"Clever, aren't you?" he said, sarcastically. He pointed a pistol at her.

Good grief.

"Well, you're not going to tell the tale to anyone else," he said through clenched teeth.

"Oh, I don't think so. The police are already here," she bluffed.

Earlier she had dialed 9-1-1, discreetly while fiddling in her purse. She hoped they were listening.

Moments later, sirens sounded in the background.

She breathed a sigh of relief. Well, thank God for that.

**

"How did you figure that out, dear niece?" Aunt Edna asked.

"Well, he told me his neighbor once teased him that he had no friends and no one liked him. I guess he wanted to prove to his neighbor wrong. He arranged to have all these 'fake' guests at his funeral to prove he was someone and that he was well popular."

"Pity, he didn't take the effort to make real friends in real life though."

"Oh, that's not always easy."

"So Pete was a detective then who was in on this paid guest thing?"

"I guess it's not so much the service as the particular client using it as a scam to milk the person paying them."

"I see."

"So what is this paid guest business?" Aunt Edna said.

"Her website listed her gigs as an actress. She certainly gave a lot of information about what she did for a living online. I looked at all the people involved...followed the money. It was Kel, the head usher at the memorial home who enlisted her for this gig. He told Mr. Lion that he could get him paid mourners to beef up his image after death?"

"That's absurd!"

"Not really. Professional mourning or paid mourning is an occupation that originates from Egypt, China and many other cultures. Professional mourners have a name too. They're also called moirologists or mutes and they're compensated to deliver a eulogy or help comfort and entertain the grieving family."

"You mean rent-a-mourner?"

"I guess you could say that. Seems to me it's easier for some people to make money than to make friends. I guess Mr. Lions was one of those people."

"Who knows?"

"His one mistake is making the wrong person know that he had no real friends or family. Never let people know too much about your business or whether or not you'd be missed if you were...well, you know."

"That's true. I guess he told too much to that scammer, and that con-artist thought he could get away with it by hiring his friend to pretend to be Mr. Lion's girlfriend.'"

"Then presenting the lawyer with an updated will, which he managed to forge the signature on it."

"How awful."

"Well, crime never pays. Criminals get caught in the end. Or karma catches up with them big time. Always do good, as Grams would say, right?"

"You've got that right, darling niece. And as for that horrible head usher..."

"It would have helped if he knew enough about not double-crossing people too. He made an arrangement with his friend and she broke it. I wonder why?"

"We will never really know the truth about that, but one thing's for sure. No one, and I mean no one deserves to be murdered. Meaning, Mr. Lion's paid girlfriend guest."

"That's true. Well, crime never pays. No matter have clever the criminal tries to plot the perfect murder. You think they would learn. There's a saying you know, 'be careful what you do, because the unseen eye is watching you.' Whatever that means."

"Speaking of eyes, I saw the way that cute detective looked at your earlier today when he came by to thank you for helping him out on this case."

Heat crept to Annabelle's cheeks. "You did?"

"Yes. When are you two going out on a date?"

"Auntie, I already told you, I'm taking a break from dating right now."

"Well, don't wait too long. I think there's a bit of chemistry there."

Annabelle didn't want to mention they'd already been on a lunch date. But it was cut short by a radio call of a break in. He had to leave early. She wondered if he'd ask her out again though.

Annabelle didn't want to admit it, but her aunt was right. Annabelle felt a sweet chemistry between her and Detective Chad.

She wondered if their paths would ever cross again. Secretly, she hoped so. Under much nicer circumstances, of course.

***

Donuts and Murder: The Rich Housewife

Annabelle stumbles on a strange mystery with a bizarre twist after the death of one of her customers, a notorious rich housewife.

"All you need is love...and donuts."
- Author Unknown

The mouth-watering sweet scent of baked cinnamon wafted to Annabelle Darlin's nose as she finished adding sprinkles to a dozen donuts at the Darlin Donuts Café in Apple Cove, Ontario. The batch she was working on was scheduled be to be delivered to Mrs. Debs Palmer-Wealth wife of Eeon Wealth, one of the richest men in Apple Cove, in an hour. Mrs. Palmer-Wealth was one of her busiest customers for her catering business.

Annabelle had been catering for the Wealth family for a while now. And Mrs. Wealth always had the most extravagant parties and events at the mansion over on the east side of town.

Annabelle loved pleasing her customers and they came from all walks of life. Rich, poor, working, in between jobs. Everyone came to the Darlin Donuts Café to hang out and mingle and enjoy savoring treats from the menu.

It wasn't too long ago that Annabelle was in between jobs wondering how on earth she would make ends meet.

It turned out to be a blessing in disguise when Annabelle was suddenly laid off from her job and moved back to the small town of Apple Cove, a town of rolling green hills, apple orchards and the freshest country air you'd ever breathe in, just outside the city of Toronto. Not only did her now ex-boyfriend leave her for their boss—talk about tension mixed with heartbreak, but she escaped the hamster-wheel rat race and used some of the severance pay to open up her own small business, Darlin Donuts café. She had the pleasure of serving the finest customers and being a part of the lives of many wonderful people. Sadly, it wasn't all fun and food when bad things happened—like murder.

Annabelle finished boxing up the treats.

She still had a while to go before heading out to the Wealth Residence. Mrs. Wealth made it clear that she liked people to be on time, not a minute before or a minute late. Annabelle was not going to make *that* mistake again. She'd time herself to show up on time. When she'd arrived twenty minutes early once, Mrs. Wealth made her wait a full twenty minutes before opening up the gate to let her car through security. It was weird to say the least. Still, Mrs. Wealth wasn't a bad tipper.

She then wiped her hands on her apron and went out into the dining room.

"Are you finished with the boxes?" Aunt Gabby asked.

"Yep, they're ready to go. I think Mrs. Wealth is hosting a meeting this morning."

"She certainly hosts a lot of meetings, parties and social events, doesn't she?" Aunt Gabby said of Mrs. Wealth. "She has them almost every day!"

"Well, she can do whatever she pleases. It's her life," Annabelle said.

"I feel sorry for her staff. The trouble is, it's the help that does *all* the work."

"Not anymore. I heard she fired a lot of them," a customer said, overhearing their conversation.

"What do you mean?"

"The Wealths are mean with money. They fired most of their house staff."

"I heard it's because they don't trust anyone," another customer said. "Well, *Mrs.* Wealth doesn't trust anyone. She's a bit paranoid. She suspected the help of spying on her."

"*Spying* on her?" Annabelle asked incredulously.

"Yes, especially the housekeeper. She never liked Fannie. You know Fannie? She comes in here a lot."

"Oh, yes, right, Fannie. She's a nice lady."

"She's been the maid for over 15 years. Long before Eeon married Debs. Yet Debs just fired her for no reason."

"Fannie must be upset."

"It happened recently. She's waiting for Mr. Wealth to come back to town so he can give her a reference. Debs refuses to give her one. Saying she's a spy."

"That's awful. Where is Eeon anyway?" Annabelle queried.

"Oh, he's halfway 'round the world. He spoils his wife. She says she doesn't want to travel too far. Doesn't trust planes."

"*Okay.*" Annabelle arched a brow.

"He just spoils her and buys her anything she wants. He doesn't mind. Guess it works out for the best."

"I guess so."

"That's what happens when you have more money than you know what to do with and you're surrounded by broke people in this tough economy," the customer added. "You get paranoid. You think people are out to get you or your money. Sometimes you're better off not to have too much."

"Now that's not fair. If people work hard for what they have, what's the problem with that?" Dana asked.

"Sometimes, it's better to be a millionaire-next-door-type. You know that book. Just live the simple life while you can pay all your bills and take all the vacation you want. It's when people know you have money that's the problem."

Annabelle sighed. Maybe the customer had a point.

Oh well, she wasn't in that category. She opened up her own store after getting laid off, but she was far from rolling in the doughnut dough, so to speak. Well, not just yet. She was running into debt to keep things afloat which wasn't unusual for most new businesses.

Just then the door chime sounded and a middle-aged woman walked in.

"Well, what a coincidence," Aunt Edna said.

"What's a coincidence?" Annabelle asked.

"Look who just walked in here," she said.

Annabelle craned her neck to glance over at the door and saw a woman in a red cardigan walk in. It was Lillie Palmer. The sister of the wealthy Mrs. Palmer-Wealth.

"Fancy that. I wonder what she would say if she knew we were delivering goods to her dear sister?" Aunt Edna said.

"Probably not much."

"What's the story there?" Jack inquired as he walked over to them from the kitchen.

"Oh, it's nothing." Annabelle wanted to get back to work.

"Nothing? It's one of the biggest scandals to rock this town," Aunt Edna said. "Jack you were probably too young to know about it. But over a decade ago Lillie was engaged to Mr. Wealthy, but then her sister stole him from her."

"You can't *steal* a person, Auntie." Annabelle resisted the urge to playfully roll her eyes.

"Yes, you can. You can steal their heart. One has to be careful. Well, anyway, she claimed she was pregnant for him and he dumped her sister and married her instead."

"I thought they were a childless couple."

"She ended up losing the child. Then they adopted a child and put the kid in boarding school in Switzerland."

"Well, what's the point of having a kid if you're not going to raise them yourself?" Aunt Gabby chimed in.

"I'm sure they have a good reason, Auntie. We can't be judging people if we haven't walked a mile in their shoes."

"I think I'd get serious pain issues with my feet by the look of those narrow expensive-looking stilettos that woman wears," Aunt Edna said.

"Good morning, Ms. Palmer. What can I get for you today?" Annabelle asked, as the woman approached the counter.

"Oh, I'll have a custard-filled chocolate donut and a coffee, black, please. To stay."

"Sure thing." Annabelle put the order through. She glanced up at the clock. She would have to be leaving soon to get to Mrs. Palmer-Wealth for the delivery.

Annabelle's eyes were drawn to Ms. Lillie Palmer's wrist. There was a nasty fresh red scratch on it. It looked as if someone scraped their long nail along it and it was bleeding earlier.

"Are you all right?" Annabelle said, noticing the mark and gesturing to it. "We have a First Aid kit in the back. You should probably bandage that up."

As if self-conscious, Lillie pulled her cardigan sleeve or it to cover it up. "I'm fine, thank you."

Annabelle remembered what was said earlier about rich folks and broke people around them. Truth be told, Lillie has mentioned she'd been having trouble with her rent since being laid off recently and there's rumor that her wealthy sister, Deb, won't even help her out. Her sister who *stole* Lillie's rich fiancé from her.

A slight headache surfaced on Annabelle's forehead. She tried to ignore it.

"Lillie! Lillie, the book girl, how are you doing?" another customer said to Lillie.

"Oh, I'm...I'm fine, thank you." Lillie's eyes were downcast.

"Always has a book in her hand or an e-reader now," the older gentleman turned to Annabelle then to Lillie, "Isn't that right, Lillie?"

Lillie took the plate with her order on it from Jack who handed it to her. She did not look up.

"Hey, sorry to hear about your um...well, your job. You know you should check out the library. I think they might be hiring part time," Annabelle offered.

"Yes, I'll be going to an interview soon. It's only for one day a week though. I love being around books so I don't mind. But it's not going to pay the rent. I'll still need a full-time job with benefits."

Annabelle's heart sank when she heard that. She'd been there before. Didn't seem fair at all. Also, the fact she had her rich sister who happened to be rich because she ran off with Lillie's ex-boyfriend seemed so unfair. She wondered what they had in common. Eeon was supposed to be some sort of geek who made a lot of bank with his new app. Debs certainly was the model type but it seemed as if Lillie and Eeon would have made a better match.

Stop that Annabelle. It's none of your business why or how people choose their partners.

Annabelle loved the café as it was such a social place for people to indulge in a sweet treat while catching up with friends and neighbors but it could also be a bit of a gossip hub too and she had to be mindful of that and keep out of that line of thinking.

Later, Annabelle went out into the parking lot with her boxes of donuts for Mrs. Wealth. As she drove up the quiet road leading up to the Wealth Mansion, a car zoomed by her at lightning speed. The driver must have been way over the limit. She caught a glimpse of the driver with flamed-red hair. Wasn't that Fannie, the housekeeper, or rather the *former* housekeeper?

As soon as she pulled up to the iron gates of the mansion, a disembodied voice came over the speaker asking her to announce herself.

"My name is Annabelle Darlin from Darlin Donuts Café. I have a delivery for Mrs. Wealth."

Before long, the gates clicked open and she drove through. She glanced at the clock on the dashboard.

Thankfully, she was on time. Not too early. And definitely not late.

When she pulled up, she was stunned.

A robot machine that had the word Butler on its screen answered the door.

Okay.

This must be new.

She guessed Mrs. Wealth trusted droids over humans, especially while her husband was away. Her husband was after all a tech millionaire so what else would she expect.

Well, they were certainly saving money there. But she felt uncomfortable with the fact that it meant one more human was out of a job. She was all for technology, just not at the cost of replacing the human workforce. Then what would people do? She couldn't help but think this was why she too was downsized. Automation and technology took over her previous work.

Well, it was no surprise that people were buying those robot vacuums that could vacuum your entire living room then return back to its dock, so why not a larger one that could open doors, right? Well, she figured they had an automated lock opening device, but the robot met the guest the door.

Still, there was nothing like having a warm human touch to everything. You couldn't really replace that, could you?

"Hello? Mrs. Wealth," Annabelle called out after she entered the home.

Just then, Annabelle had an eerie feeling. The house seemed empty. Her head started to pound like a base drum again. What was that feeling?

Her footsteps tapped lightly on the marble floor as she made her way into the dining area then towards the kitchen. Since she'd been there before many times for catering, she knew to go directly to the kitchen to drop off her items. But she would often be greeted and led back there by the housekeeper, Fannie. The one she swore she saw speeding away from the house.

Just then, Annabelle froze. Her eyes widened in shock.

She dropped the donuts on the floor and screamed out.

Just outside the window, she caught a glimpse of the beautiful pool but there was a body floating on the water faced down.

**

Annabelle rushed outside to the pool when the glass sliding doors opened and she called out. But it was no use. Annabelle wasn't a swimmer. In fact, she used to make jokes with Mrs. Wealth at the time who admitted she too wasn't a swimmer either though she loved looking at her pool.

She immediately fished into her pocket for her cell phone then pressed the emergency button for 9-1-1.

Just then the gardener came rushing outside to the pool area where she stood.

Where *was* the gardener this whole time?

"Are you all right?" he asked. Then he looked into the pool. "Oh, my God! Debs!"

He called her *Debs*?

He didn't call her Mrs. Wealth, which was unusual since she insisted all the help call her Mrs. Wealth. In fact, she insisted everyone called her that. Not that there was much human help left at the home.

Annabelle guessed it was harder to find a robotic gardener so she left him working there.

Moments later, the police showed up with the forensic team.

Annabelle's head pounded and her blood roared through her veins. This was awful. How terrible. She wondered if it was an accident or...worse.

Why would Mrs. Wealth be in the pool?

She couldn't swim.

Annabelle observed the body being pulled out of the pool. Mrs. Wealth still had her heels on. Which was unusual.

Mrs. Wealth's body had a black high-heeled laced up stiletto sandals with a fastened ankle strap.

So, that would explain why she was still wearing it when she slipped in the pool—or was pushed!

The sandals were secured to her feet and could not easily slide off.

Still, Annabelle couldn't help but wonder whom Mrs. Wealth was planning to meet. Was it a female guest or a male guest? Why wear stilettos by the pool?

Annabelle just had that sinking feeling that this incident was foul play. Her gut instinct told her so. Which led her to another observation. Who on earth would wear that while reading at the pool side? It looked as if Mrs. Wealth was going to be meeting someone there.

Well, duh?

She had a book club meeting soon. That must be *some* book club. Annabelle knew Mrs. Wealth liked to meet with other fashion socialites so maybe they all dressed up for their book club reading.

She obviously fell in or slipped in. Her sun hat was floating in the pool nearby.

What an awful scene. The lounge chair was nearby with a book on it. So she must have been reading as usual by the pool.

But how did she get in there?

Annabelle also noticed a long gash across the Mrs. Wealth's neck. As if she'd been in a cat fight. A similar scratch that appeared on her sister Lillie earlier at the café, Annabelle thought to herself.

"Ms. Darlin," Detective Chad MaGuire said as he approached Annabelle.

He'd just been over by the pool by the Mrs. Wealth's body examining the area with his team.

Oh, there he was again. What must he think seeing her there at the scene of another incident involving a dead body.

Still, her heart turned over in her chest whenever he was nearby. She didn't know why. The man had that effect on her. He was just so tall and gorgeous. But meeting up under these circumstances was not a good thing.

"Morning Detective. I can just imagine what you must be thinking."

"What would that be?" He arched his brow.

"How we're always meeting under these circumstances," she said, gesturing around. "It's so sad."

"Yes, it is. The Wealths are good people."

Not everyone thinks so.

"Yes, they are. Have you managed to reach Mr. Wealth?"

"He'll be in town soon. His plane just landed."

"Oh, dear." Annabelle could just imagine how he would react once he found out his wife was dead. A freak accident. Or possibly murder.

Why did that thought slide through Annabelle's mind?

She just felt that something was very odd about this whole situation.

Mrs. Wealth always read by the pool. Did she suddenly slip in?

"I understand it was you that found the body?" the detective said, pulling out his notepad. That very familiar notepad with the brown leather cover. Oh, dear. How many times had Annabelle seen that notepad? Looked as if he was due for an upgrade, since it looked so worn and torn. Much like he did.

He was handsome, a rugged handsome, but looked as if he'd just worked a double shift and could use a good night sleep.

"Yes, I came in to deliver her donuts for her meeting this morning. I was buzzed through by security. Well, by the automated security."

"Oh, right. It's a pretty high-tech place they've got going." He scribbled down some notes on his pad.

"Yes, well, that's no surprise since Mr. Wealth specializes in that." She looked around hugging herself. She felt a sudden chill come over her. Something did not seem right.

"What happened to all the staff?" the detective asked.

"As you know, the gardener was the only one left. He didn't know she was in the pool or near the pool. He told me he'd just come to cut the grass as usual and that's when he saw us."

"I see," Detective Chad scribbled down some more notes on his pad.

"Did Mrs. Wealth say *who* she was meeting this morning?"

Annabelle shook her head. "No. Unfortunately not. I wish I knew who she was meeting this week."

"This week?"

"Yes, she's always hosting events or having meetings. She books her catering in advance."

"And she didn't tell you anything about her event this morning?"

"Nothing at all, Detective."

Annabelle thought for a moment. Should she tell the detective about Mrs. Wealth's attire? Well, clearly they could see what she was wearing. A skimpy bikini and coverup with a sun hat and stilettos. One would wonder about the formality of the meeting. Was it a friend or just a business acquaintance?

"Did you see anything suspicious when you came in?"

"Not unless you count the fact that the place seemed quiet."

"Quiet?"

"Yes, well, she used to have a lot of staff around here. But I heard she fired them recently. The Wealths prefer to automate almost everything now."

"I see," he said, jotting down notes on his notepad.

Annabelle could not believe the events of the day. It all seemed so surreal.

Mrs. Wealth was dead!

She was *dead*!

"At what time did you see the body?" the hot detective interrupted her thoughts.

"It was around ten o'clock or shortly after. I arrived in time for the delivery and as soon as I came into the kitchen with the donuts I...I looked out the window and..." Annabelle almost choked with emotion.

Actually, she'd dropped the box of donuts when she saw the body floating in the pool.

She then told the detective that she dropped the donuts when she saw the body outside.

It was a horrible scene. She didn't expect to see one of her regular customers, Mrs. Wealth, floating face down in the sparkling blue pool.

Reliving that moment caused Annabelle's heart to jolt.

"It's okay, Ms. Darlin. Take your time," Detective Chad said soothingly, understanding the emotion she was going through.

Annabelle finished explaining the events of that morning including the gardener coming out to help and calling the police.

"You've been helpful, Ms. Darlin," he said, wrapping up his notes and closing his notepad. "If you think of anything else, please notify us."

"Will do, Detective."

It seemed as if she was always having that conversation with Detective Chad. They were always meeting up like this—on the scene of a suspicious death!

Annabelle glanced around but something caught her attention on the ground. She saw something red on the poolside deck.

"Did the forensic team see this?" Annabelle reached to pick it up and then changed her mind. She didn't want to tamper with evidence.

"Don't touch that." He saw what she was looking at and went over to the area.

"Oh, no. I wasn't going to." Annabelle knew all too well not to mess with a scene of an incident.

He called for his team to look at the article on the ground. They carefully picked it up and bagged it. It looked like a broken nail. One of those long fake nails with bright red sparkling nail polish on it.

Annabelle thought for a moment.

Whose fake nail was that?

Did it belong to Mrs. Wealth?

Or her visitor?

Or her killer?

**

"Isn't that awful?" Aunt Gabby said to Annabelle later that afternoon at the café. The news had already circulated around town.

"You're telling me." Annabelle thought for a moment. She also thought about Mr. Wealth. Poor little rich man. He just lost his wife.

"She'd just called me this morning to confirm the delivery," Annabelle said, "and then in that short period of time between then and the delivery—she was gone!"

Annabelle was still shaken up over the entire incident. While everyone in the dining room talked about the events of the morning, the breaking news came on the TV screen. All eyes were glued to the screen. Annabelle's heart raced. She drew in a deep breath. This was not good. Not good at all.

"The body of one of Apple Cove's wealthiest housewives was found in the pool by her caterer..." as the reporter talked, Annabelle couldn't help but feel all eyes shift to where she was standing.

Okay. Now would be a good time to exit the dining area.

"I'll just be in the back, checking on the donuts," she said before excusing herself.

When she went to the kitchen through the swinging doors, she glanced out the window and thought she saw Mr. Wealth pull up in the parking lot opposite the café. She immediately took her apron off and went outside.

"Mr. Wealth." She tried to call out to him. She wanted to offer her condolence to him in person. Especially given that she'd found his wife dead. What must he be going through? He looked beaten down. He was alone when he got out of the car. No doubt, having just travelled and gotten off the plane after a long flight.

Just then, something flew past her head and almost caused her to stumble.

Uh-oh.

It was one of those annoying drone toys.

"Stop that!" she heard a woman call out. Then she heard the sound of a youngster.

"It's just for fun."

Soon the woman and the young boy came around the corner.

"Sorry about that," the woman said apologetically.

"No problem." She ducked while the drone toy zoomed back to the owner.

"He just got it and he's trying to control it."

"Oh, right. One of those things, eh?" Annabelle said, trying to be polite. She recognized the woman as a customer of the café. And the boy was her son.

"That thing is dangerous, be careful where you fly it, son," Annabelle said.

"Sorry."

Annabelle looked again and saw Mr. Wealth had gotten back into his car and driven off.

Oh no. She wanted to talk to him.

It looked as if he was at the pharmacy, a few doors down from the café in the plaza, probably getting something to help calm his nerves.

But she missed her chance to talk to him. She'd have to speak to him later.

"Everything all right?" Her aunt said, coming outside.

"Oh, I just saw Mr. Wealth."

"Out here?"

"No over there. A few doors down. He was at the pharmacy. Looked like he just picked up something small."

"I see."

Annabelle thought for a moment. His wife just died. He decided to go to the pharmacy? *Hmm*.

"I see the wheels turning in your head, dear niece. What is it?"

"Something seems a bit off."

"Yes, I know what you mean. It's always the husband, right? But it looks like a simple accident."

Was it though?

**

Later that night at home by the fireplace, Annabelle and her two aunts discussed the events of the day.

"It must have been the sister?" Her aunt said, biting into a crispy chocolate frosted donut filled with vanilla cream.

"Why do you say that?" Annabelle asked.

"She lost her beau to her sister. And what about that nail you saw at the scene?"

"But why would she get revenge now? Of all times?"

"She does have a point, Aunt Gabby." Annabelle thought for a moment." She had the motive for sure."

"True. But what about the means?" her aunt asked.

"That's the thing. There was no sign of anyone having been there around the time she...slipped into the pool."

"Do you think it was suicide?" Aunt Gabby said.

Aunt Edna rolled her eyes. "My dear sister, do you ever *think*?"

"Aunt Edna!" Annabelle always ended up refereeing between the two sisters.

"What? Why on earth would a woman dress up, go to the poolside and order a tray of donuts then plunge herself in the pool?" Aunt Edna said.

Aunt Gabby looked sheepish. "Fine. Do you have any other ideas?"

"I think it was so strange that the gardener happened to be there?" Annabelle said.

"Why do you think that's strange? You don't expect her to do her own gardening, do you?" Aunt Edna quipped.

"No, no. Not that. It's just that...well, I found it strange that he addressed her by her first name, a shortened version of her first name. To me it suggests a bit of intimacy. I mean no one addresses her that way."

"That's true. She's a bit standoffish. She insists her entire staff calls her Mrs. Wealth."

"Do you think it was the husband then? It's always the next of kin who's the main suspect."

"He was far away," Aunt Edna said, rolling her eyes.

"Although, he could have hired someone to do it," Annabelle added, feeling an uneasy feeling. Was she far off?

"That's true. But then people always talk, don't they? There's no way he would do that and have someone out there holding that over him. You can't get away with much these days. Stuff always gets leaked online."

"True."

"So what do you think happened? Was it just an accident?"

"I don't think so. Every time I hear the word accident, my head hurts," Annabelle said.

"That means you need to get some sleep, darling. You overthink too much."

Annabelle playfully rolled her eyes. "Thanks, auntie. But I don't think it's sleep that I need. It's the missing piece to this puzzle.

Mrs. Wealth did *not* have an accident."

Annabelle stood up.

"Where are you going?" her aunt asked.

"I need to look something up."

"Oh dear, not Google again."

"No. No. It's not just that. Well, everyone has a social media page."

"Not me," Aunt Edna said. She leaned back and began knitting a new orange cardigan. She believed everyone needed a cardigan. She always had to be doing something with her hands.

"*Oh*, oh, you should try it," Aunt Gabby added. "It's *so* much fun. You get to keep in touch with people you haven't seen in a while. I have five hundred followers."

"Do you actually *know* any of them?" Aunt Edna stopped knitting for a moment and arched a brow, peering over her dark-rimmed glasses.

Aunt Gabby looked a bit deflated and had a funny frown on her face. "That's not the point."

"What *is* the point then?" Aunt Edna continued with a grin then rolled her eyes.

"Okay, aunties," Annabelle interjected. "Please don't argue."

"We're not arguing." Aunt Edna continued to knit.

"Speak for yourself," Aunt Gabby said, biting into another donut, sipping her tea, her cell phone in one hand as she continued to scroll her feeds.

"I just want to look something up," Annabelle said, pulling out her tablet, swiping the screen. She loved how easy it was to access the Internet. The world was at her fingertips.

"So far, I need to find out everything I can about the housekeeper, Fannie," Annabelle said. "She could not have been too happy being let go. And then there's the gardener. And then Lillie Palmer, her sister. Hell hath no fury than a woman scorned and having to watch her ex-beau marry her sister and live happily ever after couldn't be easy."

"That's not what the English poet and playwright William Congreve wrote in 1697."

"No, it isn't I added the last part, of course, but you get the drift."

Annabelle spent the next few hours looking at profiles and fact checking the information on profiles of everyone in Mrs. Wealth's circle, including Mr. Wealth. My, how time went by when you were searching online.

She was stunned at what she saw. Or what she didn't see. She jotted down some information on her notepad. She was going to have a good chat with Detective Chad soon.

✱✱

The following week, Annabelle saw Lillie Palmer at the grocery store. She was about to go over to the aisle to offer her condolence when...The gardener approached Lillie.

Lillie then looked around as if to see if they were being watched. Then...

Lillie and the gardener walked out of the store together.

What was going on?

Annabelle dropped her items in the cart and walked quickly, trying to follow them.

She eyed them through the glass of the grocery store.

"Oh, my goodness. They *know* each other?"

That didn't sit too well with Annabelle at all.

Were they in on this together?

Did Lillie plot to kill her sister, using the gardener.

✱✱

Later that afternoon, Annabelle shared her observations with Detective Chad. He probably thought she was just there to distract him from his work. Truth was, she could have called him, but...okay, she was mildly attracted to him, but nothing could ever come of it.

She was on a break from dating right now. Her ex-husband had left her after all for another woman. She was not ready to put her heart back out there again. Not yet. But there was no harm in being around adorable men, was there?

He shook his head while seated behind the desk in his office. "There was no sign of forceable entry, Annabelle," Detective Chad said to her. "She was alone."

"Yes, but have you looked at the gardener? He had the entry code to get in and out and well, he was *there*."

Chad leaned back in his chair, giving Annabelle a grin. "I'm sorry, Annabelle, you've been very helpful on the last few cases here, but I'm afraid this was just a simple accident."

"But how could it be? I...I don't know how to explain this, but I just have a feeling."

"I'm afraid having a feeling is not enough to arrest someone. We go by facts."

"I think she was pushed."

"By what, a puff of air?"

"Excuse me?"

"Annabelle, we checked out all the cameras in the area. According to the footage we have in the area and around the house, she was alone. She simply slipped and fell into the pool." Chad gave her a raised brow. "But I see you're not satisfied with that."

"No. I'm not. I get a slight uneasy feeling when something's off, like a sixth sense or something. Or more like a seventh sense that something is wrong. Then my head starts to pound as if someone or something is knocking on my skull trying to get in, to show me the answer."

He looked at her with a grin, his eyebrow still arched.

"Okay, I know that doesn't make sense, but..."

"Annabelle, a tourist in the area come forth with a video," he said. "She was filming a video near the mansion with her cell phone between 9:48am to 9:58 am, the approximate time of the accident. Now, that coincides with every other camera. She even has the sound on the video. She heard the splash. But there was no one there. Then you pulled up at the gate. It was all caught on camera."

Annabelle's stomach tightened.

That just didn't make any sense.

"Can I please see the video?" she asked the detective.

"Annabelle, you know I can't do that."

"I just want to help you, Detective. Please. I was there. I have the right to see it. I was in the video, after all."

"Fine then. Just this once."

Annabelle looked at the video over and over again. The footage was taken outside the fenced area. She listened carefully to the sounds in the video. But then something struck her as odd.

**

Later that afternoon, Annabelle went back to the mansion. "I'm so sorry to trouble you," she said to the gardener who opened the door.

"Hey, no worries. I was just packing up the rest of my stuff."

She noticed he had a suitcase and a duffle bagged slugged over his left shoulder.

"You mean, Mr. Wealth is not keeping you on?"

"Oh, no. He wants to sell the place."

"He does?" Annabelle was puzzled. "That's too bad. It's such a beautiful mansion, but I understand the memories of...well, what happened."

"It's crazy though. Mrs. Wealth wanted this home. He always wanted to sell it, but she wouldn't let him."

"Oh?"

Annabelle wanted to ask him about his relationship with Mrs. Wealth's sister, but she stopped herself.

"Where is Mr. Wealth now?" she asked, instead.

"In his lab as usual."

"His lab?"

"Yes, his computer lab down the hall near the study."

"Thank you. I'm going to see him now. And...well, I wish you luck."

"Thanks," he said, not looking at her. She watched as he made his way out the door and then down the driveway.

Annabelle then made her way down the hallway towards the study. She looked inside the study and noticed that the painting on the wall of Mrs. Wealth had been taken down. It was placed on the ground leaning on the wall by the fireplace.

She walked into the study, stunned.

Who could have done that?

And why?

She reached into her purse and pulled out her cell phone and took a picture of the painting on the ground.

"Can I help you?"

She spun around, startled.

It was Mr. Wealth.

She slid her phone back into her purse.

"Oh, Mr. Wealth, sorry. I was...I just wanted to offer my condolence in person."

He looked at her skeptically—his eyes travelled to her purse slung across her shoulder.

"And you are?"

"Annabelle from...from Darlin Donuts. I...I discovered your wife's body in the pool. I'm so sorry about what happened."

"Yes, it was an unfortunate accident." His tone was set.

"It was unfortunate, but I don't think it was an accident."

"Excuse me?"

"Why did you do it, Mr. Wealth?"

"Do what? What are you talking about?" His eyes narrowed with anger.

"You killed your wife."

He shook his head. "Get out of my house."

"It's not your house, Mr. Wealth. And you know what I'm talking about."

"First of all, Ms. Darlin, I was not here when my wife had her unfortunate accident."

"No, but you didn't have to be."

"What?" She saw his Adam's Apple bub up and down in this throat.

"You see I thought it was strange that no one was around at that time and well, she was expecting someone, her gardener to come in. If they were having an affair, you could have divorced her on the grounds of infidelity. But she wasn't. The gardener was her half-brother. Her ex-convict half-brother. She wanted to help him out. And he assumed another name. But that wasn't it. You wanted her out of the way, because you didn't want to split your fortune."

"What are you getting at?"

"The truth, Mr. Wealth. The truth."

"The truth is my wife died after she slipped into the pool. There's nothing more to it. And you need to leave or I'll call the police."

"I'm sure you won't do that." Annabelle tried to keep her wits together.

"You see you killed your wife and I can prove it."

"How?"

How was not the word she was expecting from him. She knew he was guilty but would her plan work?

She reached into her purse and pulled out a small remote control. She'd borrowed it from that customer's son she met the other day for this experiment. She clicked a button on the device.

Then the small toy drone that she'd placed on the counter when she first walked in lifted off the ground and into the air. It then went over to Mr. Wealth.

He practically swatted the thing away after docking.

"Are you crazy? What are you doing? You're mad!"

"No, you are, Mr. Wealth." She then commanded the drone to return to its spot.

She walked over to the robot in the corner of the study and showed him the mark on the bottom.

"You see, I was almost run over by this little thing. And then it dawned on me later. You could be almost anywhere controlling this type of dangerous machine. Even at the airport."

"What?"

"Then I noticed the day of the so-called accident, the robot had red varnish paint on it. And then there was a broken nail on the ground. It was Mrs. Wealth's. The robot had come towards her full speed and she tried to stop it and broke her nail on it, before it managed to push her into the pool at the deep end."

"Robots can't operate on their own."

"Exactly. They need a remote control. Like this one." She showed him the device in her hand. "Mrs. Wealth has a copy, and so you do? And you know who else has a copy? Fannie—your mistress. The one you hired as your housekeeper."

He looked stunned, angered.

He clenched his teeth.

"You can't prove a thing." He pulled out a small pistol. "And you *won't*."

"You're going to just shoot me?" Her eyes widened in shock.

Just then police sirens blazed from outside.

"I've been recording the whole thing on my cell phone, Mr. Wealth. And the police have been listening in. It's over."

**

"How did you know?" Detective Chad said to her later that evening.

"I knew she was pushed. The nail on the ground was her own after she defended herself but from whom...or what? That came to me later when I almost got hit by a toy drone. And of course, Mr. Wealth made his fortune in high tech toys, didn't he? After all, it was a robot that answered the door to me that morning. I realized that Mrs. Wealth had the controls but so did her husband. He also had a controller that was remote. He made sure of it so that anyone of them could work the robotics in the home."

"Wow, you are amazing, you know that?"

"Thank you."

"How did I let you convince me again to put yourself in danger?" He then added. "You could have been killed."

"But I wasn't. Besides, thanks for trusting me on this one. I had to prove a point. Mr. Wealth is a powerful and rich man with connections, but I know he wouldn't do anything out in the open because his reputation would be at stake. I had to come back and make sure there was someone else in the home. I knew the gardener would be there then, though I had no idea he just got fired. Anyway, that was the only way. And thanks for being nearby."

"I would have it no other way. I don't want to see you get hurt. It's very dangerous out there, Annabelle."

"It's just that...well, my customers are like my family. And having seen one of them, well...murdered...I have this burning desire to see justice served."

"Well, that's noble of you, but I can't emphasize enough how much I care about your safety and well-being."

Her heart fluttered in her chest.

"You do?"

His face flushed slightly. Did he just admit he cared about her? Or was that her imagination? No, she didn't mishear that. He actually cared about her. Well, maybe, only as a fellow citizen, right?

"What I mean is, well, just be careful. Wouldn't want to see anything happen to anyone in the community. Apple Cove is a nice small town with good hardworking people..." He cleared his throat.

Was he nervous around her suddenly?

Stop that line of thinking Annabelle. He's just being a good detective.

"Well, I'll see you around, hopefully under better circumstances. I mean...well, at the donut shop or...well..." Now she was getting all tongue-tied.

"It's okay. Listen it's been a long day. Let me take you home."

"Sure."

"Come to think of it, I haven't had anything to eat yet. I was thinking of grabbing a bite. You hungry?"

"Are you asking me to dinner?"

"Maybe."

"Well, in that case, I accept."

There could be no harm in two citizens going to dinner, could there?

He'd asked her for lunch before but had to cut it short after receiving an emergency call. Still, she was glad to be in his company, no matter how long it was.

Maybe, it wasn't such a bad idea moving to Apple Cove after all.

***

Donuts and Murder: Death by Obituary

When one of her customers is killed by a crossbow, Annabelle Darlin wants to help the cops find the killer as she races against the kitchen timer to find out who did it.

***

"Are you all right?" Annabelle Darlin asked Mandarine Junkson, one of her regular customers. Mandarine just came in for her usual order of custard-filled donuts. In all the years she frequented the café, Mandarine had always been bubbly. But not this morning. What could have possibly burst her bubble?

Mandarine looked frazzled as if she didn't get a good night's sleep.

Annabelle wanted to reach out to her.

Annabelle loved working for herself and escaping the uncertainty and toxic rat race of the corporate world, but she had to get used to working 70 hours a week for herself so she didn't have to work 40 hours a week for someone else.

It turned out to be a blessing in disguise when Annabelle was suddenly laid off from her job and moved back to the small town of Apple Cove, a town of rolling green hills, apple orchards and the freshest country air you'd ever breathe in, just outside the city of Toronto. Not only did her now ex-boyfriend leave her for their boss—talk about tension mixed with heartbreak, but she escaped the hamster-wheel rat race and used some of the severance pay to open up her own small business, Darlin Donuts café. She had the pleasure of serving the finest customers and being a part of the lives of many wonderful people. Sadly, it wasn't all fun and food when bad things happened—like murder.

Still, she loved the sweet cinnamon scent of oven-baked or crispy fried donuts and freshly brewed coffee that wafted to her nostrils from the café kitchen and the lively chatter and laughter of her customers as they came in to enjoy a breakfast or lunch with friends.

"Not really," Mandarine said, plopping her handbag on the counter. The scent of her perfume filled the air around them.

"What's wrong?"

"Well," she said, looking around the café. "I think I'm being stalked."

"Stalked? By whom?" Annabelle asked alarmed.

"I don't know," she said, biting down on her lower lip and looking around again. "Listen, I'll get my custard-filled donuts to go this morning, please."

"Sure thing." Annabelle rang up her order then cancelled it. She called out to Aunt Gabby who was working in the kitchen this morning to put some fresh custard-filled donuts in a box.

"You cancelled the order," Mandarine noticed.

"It's on the house this morning."

"Oh, no. I can't do that."

"Listen, it's no trouble. You don't seem yourself this morning." Annabelle tried not to pry too much but she wondered if this had anything to do with Mandarine's ex-boyfriend. Mandarine often spoken of him as if she was terrified of him. Annabelle didn't want to pry but if this was a domestic situation, it was everybody's business to help or at least encourage a person to get help.

If her Aunt Gabby or Aunt Edna, her fraternal twin aunts who helped her out at the café, found out she was giving away free donuts, they'd chastise her and tell her she'd go broke at the rate she was going. But she just couldn't help herself sometimes. It was nice to not always think of the bottom line. Well, okay, maybe it wasn't good business sense, but she always trusted her gut. And her gut was telling her to cut this lady a break. Anyone who had ex-boyfriend troubles or ex-partner troubles could use a little break. She knew what *that* was like. Her ex left her for their boss and came to her café, a while back, to announce their engagement. Oh, well. Water under the bridge now.

"Here you go," Aunt Gabby said, as she walked through the swinging kitchen doors. "All boxed up and ready to go."

"Thanks Aunt Gabby," Annabelle said.

"Thank you." Mandarine's voice was soft.

"Oh, Mandarine," Aunt Gabby said. "How *are* you this morning?"

Mandarine bit down on her lower lip again and said nothing.

"Oh, that good, eh?" Aunt Gabby said.

"Auntie." Annabelle had to get used to Aunt Gabby talking first before thinking.

"What is it dear?" Aunt Gabby seemed clueless at the moment.

Just then Aunt Edna called out for Aunt Gabby.

Annabelle was so grateful to have her aunts helping her out at the café. Though they insisted since they were retired and, in their own words, getting bored out of their minds and wanted to get involved with the family business.

Annabelle made sure to pay them well, just like the other staffers, though they'd argued with her about it. But she told them she just wouldn't have any volunteers in the store. Everyone got paid well for their work. And the fast food business wasn't the easy food business. When it got busy, it got *busy*.

"Would you like to talk?" Annabelle offered after Aunt Gabby went back to the kitchen. "Privately?" she added.

"Yes. Uh...sure..."

Annabelle and Mandarine found a quiet booth near the kitchen away from the other customers.

"Is everything all right?" Annabelle asked again.

"Well, no. Not exactly. I'm...I'm thinking of leaving."

"Leaving?"

"Yes. Leaving Apple Cove."

"But you said you loved it here."

"I know. It's been my home for the past few years. And you guys have been amazing but..." she twisted the ring on her finger.

"Has your ex been bothering you?" Annabelle asked, concerned.

"Well..."

"It's all right, you can tell me. You know you shouldn't keep this to yourself."

She ran her fingers around the sides of the box of donuts she ordered. "Listen, I just have to go. You guys have been great and everything, but I think I'm just going to move again."

"Mandarine, what's made you so terrified?"

Mandarine looked around again then she stopped toying with the box of donuts and slipped her hand in her purse to pull out her cell phone.

"This. This is bothering me. Some cruel evil joke."

Annabelle glanced at the screen and her jaw fell open. "Are you sure it's about you? I mean your name is unusual but..."

"Yes, it's me. Same date of birth and everything." Her lips quivered then thinned into a hard line. "I wish I could kill the creep who did this."

Her tone was hard. Annabelle had never heard her speak like *that* before. Then again, how well could you know your customers?

Annabelle studied the screen again. Luckily, it was one of those large smartphones with the massive screens. There it was, on the screen as clear as day.

Obituary: Mandarine C. Junkson passed away December 12th. She was a resident of Apple Cove...

Annabelle read the rest of the obituary. It was beautifully written, but a horrible gesture. "Who would place your name in the obituary? That seems like such a sick joke. If this is your ex, you really need to contact the police about this. Not the emergency but maybe visit the police station. Is that your date of birth?"

"Yes, yes. Everything is the same. Even the town."

Annabelle knew Apple Cove was a small enough town and was willing to bet she was the only Mandarine Junkson there.

"What are you going to do about it?"

"Leave."

"But isn't that drastic? Do you think it's a threat? Or maybe a bad practical joke?"

She sighed and got up abruptly. "Listen, it was nice knowing you, but I...I'm leaving."

Annabelle knew that Mandarine fled from somewhere else when she came to town years ago. When she first started coming to the café she mentioned she had a terrible controlling ex who threatened her at times and she would leave him. But she didn't mention anything else about him.

She wouldn't talk about her family or anyone. She mostly kept to herself.

She wanted to tell Mandarine to call her anytime if she needed any help, but Mandarine was gone. She flew out of there faster than an eagle.

Just then, Annabelle got up and before she could make it to the kitchen to help out with the next batch of donuts, she heard screams from outside.

She rushed to the sound of the commotion and ran outside.

There was Mandarine on the ground, the box of custard-filled donuts splayed about on the ground beside her.

Annabelle rushed to her side. But it was too late. She checked her carotid artery at the side of Mandarine's neck. No pulse.

She heard the screeching sound of tires that drove away from the scene and looked up. She caught a quick glimpse of the vehicle speeding away.

All she could tell was that it was a white car. She couldn't tell the make or model. Darn! She wished she had a photographic memory to capture the plates.

Judging by the wound and the position of the body, she didn't think CPR would help and she didn't want to risk moving the body with the large impaled object sticking out of the back.

Mandarine was dead. There was no two ways about it. She was slumped over in the parking lot with what looked like an arrow protruding from her back.

From a crossbow?

Was that a *crossbow*?

Annabelle couldn't be sure, but it looked like it. She remembered seeing one recently at an art gallery. Who would have such an instrument? She reached down to call 9-1-1 oblivious to the commotion around her.

***

Everything happened so fast. The crowds gathered around chatting amongst themselves.

Luckily, the cops were on the scene in no time.

The police station wasn't too far from the Darlin Donuts Café.

And before long that familiar yellow caution tape was around the area when the crime scene technicians arrived.

Annabelle saw the handsome Detective Chad MaGuire interviewing one of the witnesses outside.

"How terrible," a customer said to another.

"What is this town coming to?" another quipped.

Yes, Annabelle wondered too.

This was supposed to be a nice quiet town. She'd come here to open up her donut shop away from the big city. She thought she left the big city crime behind. But so far, they'd been a few murders since she arrived. Not good at all.

Before long people had their smartphones up in the air recording what was left of the tragic incident. It seemed like a scene out of a movie rather than reality.

"This is not good," Aunt Edna said, shaking her head in dismay. "Who would do such a thing?"

"I don't know," Annabelle said as a wave of sorrow and disappointment swept over her. She wished she knew more about what was troubling Mandarine.

Did her ex kill her?

Was he the one responsible for what just transpired?

Moments later, after Aunt Edna went back to the café to help the customers and keep things going, the detective approached Annabelle.

"Good morning, Annabelle." Detective Chad greeted her.

He was a gorgeous tall and dark handsome man, but this morning she could tell when he was doing a double shift. He'd told her once that they were always short-staffed due to budget cuts. Lack of sleep was the way human's recharged. It wasn't good if that was cut back. One's skin becomes imbalanced, leading to a dehydrated complexion and sometimes redness.

Lack of sleep could really do a number on your skin if you weren't careful—not to mention your overall health. She'd read somewhere that not getting enough-sleep that is, decreases the moisture levels of your skin and lowers your complexion's pH levels, which in turn causes skin to look dull and aged.

In fact, that was just how Mandarine looked this morning too. She hadn't had much sleep either. Whoever did this was haunting her for some time. The obituary may have been the straw that broke the camel's back. But why go to the extreme level of taunting?

"Morning, Detective. Sorry we have to meet under these circumstances." Again, she wanted to add, but decided not to.

He sighed deeply. "Yes, it's tragic what happened," he told her.

"I understand you were a witness to the incident."

"Well, yes. Sort of."

"Can you tell me what happened?"

"Well, Mandarine came in this morning but she wasn't herself."

"What do you mean she wasn't herself?"

Annabelle thought of what Mandarine told her. "She was distraught. I'd say terrified. She was fearful of her life. She told me she was afraid of her ex."

He pulled out his notepad and began jotting down notes. "Did she tell you why? Did she give you his name?"

"No. She refused to."

"She refused?" he asked, puzzled.

"Yes, I tried to probe for more information. She only told me that she was planning on leaving town."

"Leaving town? Did she tell you why?"

"Well, she thought he might have caught up to her. She's usually very bubbly whenever she comes in here in the mornings for her coffee and donuts. But this morning, she looked terrified."

There was a newspaper stand nearby. Annabelle placed a coin into the box and took a copy of the *Apple Cove Newspaper* and opened it to the Obituary page.

"See here," she said, pointing to the section where Mandarine's name appeared.

He ran his fingers through his hair. "Are you sure that's her?"

"Yes, she said it was her, but obviously it was some sort of cruel joke. I asked her who could have or who would have done this, but she refused to say."

"Hmm." He took the paper from Annabelle.

Just then, another officer interrupted them. "We've got him."

"Who?"

"The driver that sped off. Witnesses gave a description of the vehicle. He ran into a pole down the street. He's in custody."

"Do you have a name?"

"Looks like it's the ex-boyfriend. He admitted that he was only trying to get in contact with her. But he won't say anything else."

"Good. I'll be right there."

Annabelle felt a tingling sensation slide down her spine. They have the wrong guy. She just felt it. Which was weird, because prior to the murder, she thought otherwise.

"You've been most helpful, Ms. Darlin."

"Please, call me Annabelle."

"Annabelle. Thank you for your time. If you think of anything else, please notify us."

"Will do, Detective."

He rubbed his gorgeous stubble. She could tell he was exhausted. Officers and detectives worked overtime at the station. Short staffing and budget issues with the small town was a concern. She was willing to bet he'd done a double. A twenty-four hour shift.

She wished she could be of more help.

Her father was an officer down south who died in the line of duty. He'd been working a double shift too and should have gotten a ride home but he figured erroneously that since he lived close by to home, it wouldn't be a big deal. He was exhausted when he'd been killed—driving and falling asleep behind the wheel. He'd driven off a cliff. The vision stuck with her in her mind all these years. She was too young to know too much about his work at the time. She was a child when he died. Was that why she was so desperate to help officers on the force too, in any small way that she could? Especially knowing that the same budgetary concerns that her father was plagued with was still happening today.

Maybe it was her own small strange way of dealing with the tragic loss. And that fact that she'd never had a chance to say goodbye. That, coupled with the fact that she had a curiosity gene and a gut instinct of solving mysteries. Much as her father did.

Much later, after Detective Chad went to speak with his colleagues, Annabelle went back outside and observed the area of the murder.

The coroner already took Mandarine's body away while the crime scene technician still worked the area. Annabelle looked around. She remembered seeing the body slouched forward. She'd been struck from behind. So it meant the cross bow came from the west side, but the driver took off from the east.

There were more than two people involved here. There had to be.

"What's on your mind?" Detective Chad asked her when he came back to the café. "I can see those wheels turning." He knew her by now.

"It's just that, well, I think there was someone else involved."

"Like who?"

"I don't know."

He just got another call on his radio. "Looks like we *do* have our killer. The ex-boyfriend confessed."

Annabelle was numb with shock. "*Confessed*? Really?"

Well, that was quick. That was way too quick. Something seemed suspicious about the whole incident. And everything happened so fast it made Annabelle's head spin.

"Yes, really. You seem surprised."

"My gut instincts are telling me it's not him, Detective."

"Really now?" Detective Chad gave her a you-can't-be-serious look.

"Did they find the murder weapon? The cross bow?"

"We'll soon find out."

"I hope you do, Detective. I think this case is a lot more complex than we can imagine."

***

Annabelle tried to trace back the steps that Mandarine took earlier when she came into the café. Was Mandarine being followed earlier?

She remembered that when Mandarine came into the café, she dumped some papers into the trash. That's not at all unusual for customers to dump stuff in there. For instance, they might have walked in off the street and had some loose papers in their pockets or old recipes. But now that Mandarine was murdered, she needed to find out what really happened to her. Her gut was telling her that the cops got the wrong person. She had told Chad that the arrow came from another direction of the car. Maybe Mandarine's ex had an accomplice, but whom?

Annabelle went outside to the trash to search through some rubbish that had been dumped there by the café earlier.

"What are you doing, dear?" Aunt Edna said, coming outside. "You know if you're hungry you can always fix something inside. No need to go digging through the garbage. Things can't be that bad," she said.

"Very funny, Aunt Edna. I'm trying to figure out what happened to Mandarine."

"In the trash, dear?"

"Not exactly. I think a clue might be in there."

"But didn't the cops arrest the boyfriend? I heard he confessed."

"The *ex*-boyfriend, but I think there's more to the case. If there's anything I've learned from mysteries is that nothing is wrapped up so easily."

"But fiction and reality are two different beasts, dear."

"And truth is always stranger than fiction, Auntie."

"Now, that is true. I can't believe she wore that awful blue and blond wig this morning."

"That's it."

"What's it?"

"She often wears a brunette wig, but you're right. This morning her wig was well, a little different from her usual. Do you think she was trying to disguise herself from her ex?"

"With a wig?"

"You're right. Besides, Mandarine dropped something in the trash. I wonder if it would be of help to the police."

"Darling, don't go meddling in the investigation."

"I'm not. I just want to help them—and to satisfy my OCD with solving crimes, especially one close to home—or close to my beloved café. She was a loyal customer, Auntie. She died on my property. I need to make sure whoever did this is brought to justice."

"Oh dear," she said, clutching her hands over her heart. "You miss your dear old dad, don't you. He always used to say he wanted to help the community and bring anyone to justice that commits a crime. You don't' remember that, but you probably heard us talk about it over the years. You think if you help the police in an investigation, you're somehow helping him."

Annabelle sighed deeply. The words went straight to her heart. "Yes, you're probably right about that. I guess it runs in the family then."

In a way, her auntie was right. It had always affected her during her childhood. As if an unresolved issue. She'd heard her father hadn't slept a wink in 24 hours. His reflex was off because of exhaustion. She knew there were some dedicated officers on the force who wanted to help but some were overworked, like her now late dad.

She was *not* going to meddle in any investigation, of course.

But she didn't want to waste their valuable time either by sending them on a wild goose chase. She needed to be sure first of what her suspicions were.

She pulled out a letter out of the trash.

"You're going to need to take a few showers after that,"
Aunt Edna turned up her nose. Ever the germaphobe.

"Yes, I know, Auntie."

"Who is that letter addressed to?"

"I don't know..." It was addressed to someone else.

Perhaps, she was going to deliver the letter to that person.
She saw it was a pre-approved credit card addressed to Laura
James.

But why throw it in the trash?

She brushed off the chocolate frosting off the white
envelope and shoved it in her handbag.

"You will take that to the police, won't you?"

"Of course." As soon as she figured out who Laura James
was and why Mandarine threw her letter out.

***

Later, Annabelle went to the Apple Cove News Agency to ask
who submitted or posted the obituary on Mandarine.

"So good to see you again, Annabelle," Paul Smith said as
she walked into the foyer of the news agency.

She enjoyed talking to her fellow Apple Cove businessman.
Paul was always a friendly neighborhood help.

They were both members of the Apple Cove Small
Business Association. He didn't have any family so he was there
most of the time at the office running things.

He used to have a serious girlfriend, but from what
Annabelle heard, it never worked out. So like Annabelle, his
business was his whole life.

"Likewise. I think it's great that businesses like you can stay in business considering the move to online these days."

"Oh, you know me, always like to keep things the way of the old. It's not easy competing with the computer world, but we do it. My grandfather started this agency, you know."

"I know." She paused for a moment. "I know this is probably confidential, but as you may have heard one of my customers, Mandarine Junkson, was killed earlier today."

"Yes, it's awful."

"But her name was in the obituary."

"It was?"

"Yes. Who runs the classified section?"

"Oh that would be Vern. Vern?" he called out to the back.

"Yes, boss." Vern came out to the front, wiping his hands on his shirt. He must have been busy working or having lunch.

"Annabelle wants to know about an obituary," Paul said. "You handle that section, don't you?"

"Yes, boss."

"Do you know who paid for the death notice?"

"Oh that obituary?"

"Yes."

"You know we don't like to operate online too much. Sure, we have a presence, but people have to come in person to pay. That's how it is here. Too many scams online. So whenever anyone comes in we have no trouble. We look it over for typos and make sure it sounds good and we print it."

"*You need to find out who posted the obituary,*" she'd told Detective Chad earlier, but the police were fixated on the cross bow confession of the ex-boyfriend.

Mandarine was her dear customer of so many years. She wanted to find out who really killed her and why.

"It was Mrs. Peeves down the street. Well, since a crime has been committed, I don't feel so bad in telling you," Vern said. "I thought it was strange that she came in and did that," he said.

"Yes, that is strange," Annabelle agreed.

"It wasn't as if she was a relative of the deceased. Well, she said it was for a friend."

"And you didn't question it?" Annabelle asked.

"Why should we? We get paid to place ads or in this case obituaries, and other notices. We get them all the time."

Later, Annabelle took it upon herself to visit Mrs. Peeves since she knew her from before. She was also a customer of the café. If Mrs. Peeves was behind this then she sure would have a problem with a cold-blooded killer on the loose and killing one of her dear customers.

Mrs. Peeves eyed Annabelle with suspicion when she came to the door later.

"Mrs. Peeves, I'm so sorry to trouble you at this time, but...I understand that you submitted an obituary notice for Mandarine Junkson."

She sighed deeply. "I don't know what you're talking about?"

"It's just that Mandarine was killed earlier."

Mrs. Peeves looked around. "Got nothing to say. That woman is trouble. *Was* terrible," she corrected herself.

"What do you mean she was trouble?"

"She's not nice. She used to take things that didn't belong to her. Take my newspapers," she said.

"So you took out an ad in the obituary as a joke?" Annabelle was stunned beyond belief.

"She deserved it. She was a horrible woman who always took what didn't belong to her. She would steal things. Steal my paper. Steal my things..."

"Grandma," her grandson came out from the kitchen. "You need to take your pills, Grandma."

"Oh, dear. Yes, that's right."

"Can I help you?" he said.

"I was just asking your grandmother here about...well, it's all right."

Annabelle felt terrible for bothering them.

She knew Mrs. Peeves could be confused a bit. But why would she submit a notice in the newspaper that her neighbor Mandarine was dead? What an awful thing to do.

Was she that upset that Mandarine might have taken her newspaper? But then again, Mandarine had someone else's letter in her handbag too.

Was Mandarine a thief? Was she a kleptomaniac? How well did Annabelle know one of her regular customers? She only knew her as a customer. Who knew what she was like behind closed doors?

Stop that, Annabelle. The woman is dead now. She can't defend herself anymore. Best to think well of the deceased.

Annabelle left the Peeves and went on her way. She was no warmer to the case being solved than before. In fact, she felt a cold chill inside her for some reason.

Did Mandarine steal Mrs. Peeves mail? She couldn't believe that in this digital age there were some communities that still received newspaper deliveries to their door.

It was a close-knit community that kept to old-fashioned ways and values. There wasn't anything wrong with that, of course. But she wondered why on earth would Mandarine take Mrs. Peeves newspapers.

It made no sense at all.

Annabelle's head began to pound. She was sensing something.

What about this Laura James character? Did Mandarine steal her mail to get her credit card information. The editor at the *Apple Cove News* mentioned about so many online scams. Was she involved in such a thing? But the question still remains...

Who shot Mandarine with a cross bow? Was it really her ex?

She couldn't believe it was.

Something was very strange about this whole situation. It gave her the creeps.

***

"Looks like people had it in for Mandarine," Aunt Edna said later.

"But that's a little creepy going so far as to put out an obituary, let her see it then kill her. Who would do that? And wouldn't they know they'd be caught by a trace to the notice placement? That is beyond creepy, Aunt Edna," Annabelle said as she placed more dough in the fryer for another batch of donuts.

Once the donuts were in the fryer. She left the kitchen staff to work on the next batch and went into her office at the back of the kitchen.

Annabelle logged in on her computer and started checking for facts online. She had to piece the puzzle together. She would hate for the real killer to be out there, running loose.

She looked up Laura James. And she was stunned at what she learned. Her eyes glared over the computer screen and the Google search results.

How could this be?

She then knew who killed Mandarine Junkson, but her question was why?

***

"How did you figure it out?" he said.

"You knew Mrs. Peeves was confused so it was easy to frame her. But the only one who placed the notice was you.

You're the only one who could have done it, but why?"

"She was an imposter. But how did you guess?"

"Well, there was the fact that she tossed out mail in *our* garbage bin. Why was she trying to get rid of it at my store? Why not at her own home? Then the addressee was Laura James."

"And?"

"Well, the woman who was killed was not Mandarine Junkson. Her real name was Laura James ...She just took on the ID of Mandarine. When I read Mandarine's obituary which happened to be a reposting of the original one five years ago, I noticed that it said she was a secretary."

"So?"

"Well, Mandarine, who was really Laura, admitted herself, she knows nothing about an office or her way around a typewriter or computer. So how was it she was a devoted secretary for 10 years with a company out west. It made no sense. I figured there must be some truth to the obituary."

"Good catch, Annabelle."

"And I remembered that you collected rare art and objects like cross bows."

"Oh, that."

"Yes, that."

"Well, you're good," he said with a smirk.

"Not good enough. I wish I could have helped Mandarine, or Laura or whatever her name was...to at least come clean. No one deserves to be murdered."

"So what about the car that drove off?"

"It was Laura's ex who was trying to meet up with her. He wanted to warn her that her father was angry"

The man before her looked straight into her eyes.

"And when he came to the café too late and saw that she'd been shot by a cross bow," Annabelle continued, "He sped off like lightning, figuring Mandarine – Laura's father or one of his hench men had done her in. Her ex already had a criminal record. There was no way he wanted to be around. But what a coward. He could have gotten her help immediately. Instead he drove off."

"Why are you telling me this?" the man asked in more of a statement than a question.

"Her father was a mobster. James James. Laura James changed her name and got a fake ID. That's why the ex-boyfriend ended up confessing thinking it was her father that took her out and he felt he'd be safer in prison for the crime than out there knowing that it might be the mobster James James."

He smirked.

"But why did you do it?"

"My fiancée. She was so beautiful. She died in a freak accident."

"I'm so sorry to hear that."

"Yes, well, she had her ID stolen and they ran up her credit cards."

"Oh no."

"Oh, yes. Well, anyway, I did what I had to do."

"But what did this have to do with Laura James? You didn't randomly take out your frustration on someone you thought was a scammer did you?"

"Ah, you are perceptive."

"Yes, you loved the real Mandarine Junkson. That was an unusual name."

"And when I saw that name on your customer-of-the-week board, I said to myself, how could it be? Then I looked her up and sure enough, she was the one. Laura stole my Mandarine's ID."

"Laura was getting away from her mobster father and a life of crime and looked up the obituary to see who died then got out a birth certificate in that person's name and with that was able to get ID in that name and start a new life—a horrible crime that, well, doesn't pay."

"What do you mean? Of course it paid."

"I don't follow you."

"Payback's a witch, Ms. Darlin. Laura used the name of my late fiancé and tried to be her. So I republished the obituary I'd written for my Mandarine so that she'd see it and know that the real Mandarine is gone. Laura died by Obituary."

"And I'm afraid, you'll be arrested by Obituary."

Just then Detective Chad came in with his team and read Paul his rights.

***

"Well, imagine that," Aunt Edna said, the following week at the house.

Aunt Edna, Aunt Gabby and Annabelle had just finished dinner and started to clear up in the kitchen.

"Laura tried to be someone else and ended up dead like them," Aunt Edna finished.

"Crazy, isn't it," Annabelle said, placing the cleaned dishes in the cupboards.

The fresh aroma of mint tea filled the air around them. They were about to have tea and biscuits in the living room by the fireplace. Their usual evening routine after a long day at work.

"Thank goodness they arrested Paul. Just when you think you know someone. Imagine committing that horrible crime." Annabelle shook her head. "I know he was heartbroken, but murder?"

"I know. I guess he wanted to be on the cover of his own newspaper," Aunt Edna said.

"So Laura's ex is off the hook?" Aunt Gabby asked.

"Not quite. He confessed to a crime he didn't commit. Obstructing justice is punishable. But that's not what has him worried."

"What has him worried?"

"His 500 parking tickets!"

"What? Five hundred?"

"Just kidding. But it may as well be. He had a *ton* of tickets and a suspended licence. I spoke with him earlier. He's getting help and wants to help out in the community. Turn a new leaf."

"Well, that's very ambitious of him," Aunt Edna quipped.

"People can change," Annabelle said.

"Speaking of which, are you going to change your mind and ask the detective out?"

"Auntie, you know me."

"Well, I'm not worried," Aunt Gabby said with a wink. "I'm sure you'll meet up again."

"Actually, I hope we don't," Annabelle said. "Not under the circumstances we've been meeting under."

They all laughed.

Still, Annabelle hoped they'd meet each other again. Under sweeter circumstances.

***

Thank you for reading a *Darlin Donuts Cozy Mini Mystery*. For more stories and information on new releases, you can connect with us at pageturningstories@gmail.com

Lightning Source UK Ltd.
Milton Keynes UK
UKHW041414291022
411313UK00006B/196